# CLOAK OF DECEPTION
by
David Dowson

www.daviddowson.com
www.daviddowson.co.uk
daraarts@sky.com

~ 0 ~

Acknowledgements
Special thanks to my mother, Beryl, who is always there for me and my sister, Jan Webber, author of the Betty Illustrated Children's books.

Other books also written by David Dowson include:

Chess for Beginners
Chess for Beginners Edition 2
Into the Realm of Chess Calculation
Nursery Rhymes
The Path of a Chess Amateur
CHESS: the BEGINNERS GUIDE eBook:

## NOVELS
Declon Five.
Dangers within
The Murder of Inspector Hine
Spooks Scarlett's Enigma
The Deception Unveiled
Webs of Blood and Shadows

## TABLE OF CONTENTS

# CHAPTER ONE

**B**ruce Logan was a guy who had always been about order and control. He'd set up his life to be just that way – quiet and in check, no room for any chaos. You could say he was the poster child for discipline and restraint.

This whole controlled gig became his signature move. But guess what? Life's got this knack for throwing curveballs when you least expect it. Bruce's grand plan and his little fortress of solitude? Well, they got demolished in one fell swoop on a fateful night.

Now, I won't bore you with unnecessary nitty-gritty of what went down that night; some mysteries are best left unsolved. But believe me, the universe decided to do a complete 180 on him.

Maybe it was a chance meeting, a lightbulb moment, or something that turned his world upside down. Whatever it was, it left its mark, and suddenly, Bruce wasn't sailing in familiar waters anymore. The old, quiet, and controlled setup didn't cut it anymore.

Picture this: It was a regular evening, and Bruce hit a local club. He figured it might help him escape his head for a while. So, there he was, perched at the bar, soaking in the lively vibes of the place. And then, out of the blue, he spots her. Pippa.

Now, let me tell you, this lady was like a walking riddle, and her name had a hint of mystery in it, too.

A magnetic force field came with her when she strolled into a room, instantly snagging everyone's attention. One thing you couldn't help but notice about Pippa was her sheer elegance. I mean, she moved through life like she was gliding on air.

Every step, every gesture wrapped up in this effortless grace that had folks watching in wonder. Pippa had this way about her that just drew you in. She was like a graceful dancer, moving through life with this breezy elegance, almost floating on air. Every little thing she did, from how she took a step to how she gestured, oozed this natural charm that left everyone around her in pure awe. Her hair, a fiery cascade of brown curls, framed her face like a work of art. The color, vibrant was a perfect match for her striking features. But it was her eyes that got you. They were this mesmerizing shade of green, like they held the answers to the universe's biggest mysteries.

You couldn't help but wonder what stories lay behind those captivating orbs. And her lips? They were this soft, rosy shade that curved into a knowing smile. It was the kind of smile that whispered of a world whole of secrets and experiences. When she spoke, it was like listening to a beautiful melody, a voice that could calm even the most troubled soul or ignite a fire in anyone lucky enough to hear it. Pippa, well, she was a puzzle, a tapestry of contradictions and intricacies. She was the kind of person who left her mark on you, a memory that lingered long after she was gone. Being around her was a reminder that there was always more to explore and discover in this world. Bruce couldn't help but be intrigued by the whole aura she had going on. He had a background in the SAS, so he had this knack for picking up on subtle stuff around him. So, he decided to approach Pippa, his curiosity in full gear. They hit it off big time like their paths were meant to cross that very night.

But here's the kicker: Pippa felt just as drawn to Bruce as he was to her. There was something in his unwavering gaze and the strength he carried that clicked with her. Bruce didn't know that Pippa had a past lurking in shadows and danger, and it was catching up with her big time.

As Bruce and Pippa spent more time together, he got wrapped up in her world, a world hiding all sorts of secrets. His military instincts kicked in, and he wanted to help her figure it out. They embarked on this wild journey together, pushing them to their limits, both physically and emotionally. For Bruce, it was a bit of a tug-of-war. He wanted to protect Pippa from whatever danger was lurking, but he also had his ghosts from the past to wrestle with. As their bond deepened, he saw Pippa hold the key to his healing, a shot at redemption he never thought possible. In this unexpected twist of fate, Bruce and Pippa found themselves leaning on each other to confront their tangled pasts, unraveling secrets and crafting a future that defied the odds.

Little did they suspect that their meeting was the start of a whirlwind adventure that would push their limits and change their lives forever. Bruce and Pippa stood at a crossroads, staring down a path that would test their courage and the depth of their connection. T

he night air was tense as Bruce was enveloped in figurative and literal darkness. Just when he

and instincts. With a final surge of adrenaline, Bruce managed to grab a moment of respite. He was battered and bloodied, breathing heavily, but he'd fought off the immediate threat. He could feel the handgun's weight in his hand, a stark reminder of his choices to stay alive. Cautiously, he crept from his hiding spot, his mind a whirlwind of thoughts. He surveyed the scene before him, the lifeless body of the assailant sprawled on the floor, their identity still obscured behind the mask. In that haunting moment, Bruce understood the close call he'd just experienced. His thoughts raced, fitting together the puzzle pieces with chilling clarity. The assailant had been hell-bent on eliminating him, driven by a hatred that remained inscrutable.

Bruce knew he couldn't afford to dawdle with the immediate threat neutralized. He had to act fast to find answers and uncover the truth concealed within this twisted web of violence. But before all else, he had to ensure Pippa's safety. As he dialed her number, a tremor of both fear and determination coursed through him. Bruce had to warn Pippa, alert her to the darkness creeping upon their lives, and shield her from the sinister forces threatening to engulf them both. The call connected, and Bruce quickly relayed the harrowing events to Pippa, his words laced with urgency as he urged her to take precautions and remain vigilant. He could sense her fear, her voice quivering as she processed the alarming news. Their conversation was brief but intense, with promises to stay safe and a mutual agreement to meet securely and strategize against the looming threat.

As Bruce hung up the phone, he couldn't shake the overwhelming weight of their situation. The assailant's brazen attack had left him with a newfound sense of urgency that throbbed in his veins. The dangerous game they had been thrust into had escalated, and they were now deeply entangled in a deadly dance, their very lives hanging in the precarious balance of a high-stakes gamble. Determined, Bruce gathered what remained of his strength and resolve. He understood they had no choice but to delve deeper into Pippa's enigmatic past. It was the only path that held the answers crucial to their survival. Their newfound partnership was forged in the crucible of adversity, and they were ready to confront the heart of the nightmarish storm that loomed ahead. Bruce walked away from the shattered window, every step filled with caution. Paranoia danced at the edges of his awareness, and he couldn't help but glance over his shoulder, his senses heightened by the threat that seemed to linger in the shadows. As he navigated the dimly lit streets, the tension never left him. His every nerve was on edge, and he couldn't shake the feeling that danger was still lurking in the corners of the night. Suddenly, a figure emerged from an alleyway, nearly brushing against him in the darkness. Instinct took over, and Bruce reacted with a lightning-fast strike, pinning the person to the ground in a swift, practiced motion. His heart raced, his muscles tense, ready to defend himself at a moment's notice. But as the seconds passed, his eyes adjusted to the dim light, revealing the truth.

The person beneath him was not an assailant but a beggar, wide-eyed and terrified. Bruce felt guilt wash over him as he realized his grave mistake. He quickly released his hold and extended a trembling hand to help the beggar to their feet. "I'm so sorry," Bruce stammered with genuine remorse. "I thought... I thought you were someone else." The beggar, shaken but unharmed, nodded and hurried away without a word. Bruce watched them disappear into the night, a deep sense of regret gnawing at him. He had allowed his paranoia to blind him momentarily, and the consequences had been all too real. Taking a deep breath, Bruce continued on his path, his senses on high alert. The night was far from over, and the dangers that lurked in the shadows were still genuine. His life was a walking tour of trouble. It has always been.

# CHAPTER TWO

A midst the wreckage of shattered windows and the echoes of gunfire, Bruce stood alone, contemplating the aftermath of the terrifying attack. It wasn't just the physical destruction that weighed heavily on him, but the disruption of doubt brewing within his mind. Pippa had been his unwavering companion throughout the perilous journey, her courage and resourcefulness drawing him closer with each passing moment. However, now, a storm of uncertainty threatened to tear their bond. Images from the attack seared into Bruce's memory, flashing vividly before his eyes. A gnawing sense of betrayal clawed at him. Did he genuinely know Pippa? Were her intentions as pure as they seemed, or was something sinister lurking beneath her façade? Bruce paced back and forth, torn between the cherished memories of camaraderie and the growing unease festering within him. He dissected their conversations, searching for hidden meanings or cryptic messages that might hint at the truth behind Pippa's motives. As time passed, the questions in his head grew more pressing and intrusive. Was Pippa somehow linked to the assailant who had attacked him? Had she, intentionally or not, led him into this treacherous journey? The unsettling suspicion coiled within Bruce's gut, chipping away at the trust he had clung to so desperately. His mind churned with conflicting thoughts as Bruce ran his fingers along the scars. He revisited their interactions, carefully dissecting Pippa's words and actions for any hints of deception. Every shared moment became a piece of evidence, analyzed for concealed motives. Yet, amid the doubt, Bruce couldn't dismiss the memories of their time together—the instances of vulnerability, the shared hardships. There were moments when Pippa had risked her safety to protect him, as well as acts of support that had seemed authentic and selfless. These gestures of kindness tugged at his heart, but the scars on his body seemed to narrate a different story. Bruce knew he couldn't keep these concerns to himself in the turmoil. Uncertainty bore down on him, threatening to smother his trust. Should he confront Pippa and risk shattering the bond they had? Or should he bury his doubts, fearing they might drive her away or provoke an unpredictable response? As Bruce grappled with his inner turmoil, he recognized that he couldn't let these doubts consume him entirely. They had faced danger together and relied on each other's strengths for survival. But now, trust had become a leap of faith, a choice between embracing suspicion or maintaining belief in Pippa. Determination coursed through him as he reached a decision. He would confront Pippa, not with accusations, but with the vulnerability of his doubts. An honest conversation was needed, a chance to lay bare their fears and uncertainties. Only then could they hope to rebuild the trust the attack had shaken. The scars etched into Bruce's body served as a reminder of the peril he had faced and the steep price he had paid for his involvement. Each mark bore the weight of his terrifying ordeal, feeding the relentless questions that tormented his thoughts. The doubts that had crept in now whispered ominous possibilities, casting a shadow over his relationship with Pippa. They owed it to each other to unearth the truth, no matter how painful it might be. Bruce sought out Pippa amidst the chaos, finding her battered yet resolute. In her eyes, he glimpsed a reflection of his concerns. In that shared vulnerability, they discovered a glimmer of hope – an opportunity to reaffirm their connection and confront the doubts threatening to drive them apart. Bruce and Pippa's meeting in their secure hideaway was fraught with palpable tension. The room, dimly lit by a single flickering light, was filled with unease that seemed to hang like a heavy curtain.

They sat across from each other at a battered wooden table, its surface marred by the scars of time. Bruce's gaze bore into Pippa, his brows furrowed with doubt and suspicion, while Pippa's eyes held a mix of apprehension and determination. The walls of the hideaway were rough-hewn, evidence of the place's clandestine nature. The air was heavy with the scent of dampness and secrecy, and the only sound was the soft hum of an old ventilation system.

Bruce began cautiously, his voice carrying the weight of his uncertainties. "Pippa," he said, his fingers tracing the rough grain of the table as he spoke, "the attack... it's got me questioning everything. I was wondering if there's more to your past. Pippa, I can't ignore these scars on my body," Bruce confessed, his voice a mixture of pain and determination. "They remind me of the danger we faced but also raise doubts. I need to know the truth. Were you in any way connected to the person who attacked me? Did you lead me into this shit hole intentionally? Because it seems like it."

Pippa's expression wavered, torn between shock and the hurt reflected in her teary eyes. "Bruce," she said, her voice quivering, "I swear to you, I had no idea this would happen. I never meant for any harm to come to you. Those scars were not my doing. I've been a victim in all this, just like you."

Pippa leaned forward, her hands trembling slightly as she tried to convey her sincerity. "Bruce, I get your doubts," she replied softly. Her gaze never left him, and she reached out to place a reassuring hand on his, the touch light yet meaningful. "My life's been complicated, and I haven't shared some things. But I promise, I've always meant well."Bruce nodded, his eyes betraying the conflict within him. "I want to believe you, Pippa," he admitted, his voice tinged with vulnerability. His gaze shifted to their intertwined hands, a silent testament to their fragile trust. "But that attack... it's left me shaken. I need to know nothing you're hiding that could hurt us."

Pippa's eyes bore into his, filled with determination and sadness. "Bruce, I never wanted any of this. I've made mistakes, and there are things I regret," she confessed, her voice unwavering. She squeezed his hand gently, a gesture meant to convey her sincerity. "But I've changed, and I'm trying to make amends. You have to trust that the person I am now is someone you can rely on. "Bruce's heart pounded in his chest as he absorbed her words. The sincerity in her voice resonated with the memories they had shared—the moments of trust and camaraderie that had once defined their relationship. The doubts that had consumed him now seemed to loosen their grip, overshadowed by the unfolding truth. He examined her face, searching for any hint of deceit or concealed truths. Yet, all he found was the earnestness etched in her features. He realized then that his doubts were rooted in fear and the shared trauma of their recent ordeal. With a deep breath, Bruce made his choice. He trusted Pippa, believing in their connection despite the lingering uncertainty.

At that moment, Bruce made a choice. He chose to place his faith in Pippa, to think that her words carried the weight of truth. The scars on his body might serve as painful reminders, but they wouldn't define their shared connection. He recognized the need to move forward, to break free from the suffocating hold of suspicion. "I believe you, Pippa," Bruce replied, his voice gentler now. "I trust that we can overcome this and find a way to move forward. But it has to be built on complete honesty, with no secrets between us. Can you promise me that?" Pippa nodded, tears streaming down her face. "I promise, Bruce," she affirmed, her voice filled with determination. "From now on, I will be completely open with you. We'll confront the truth together, no matter how challenging it may be." As they locked eyes, a fragile thread of trust began to weave back into their relationship. The doubts would take time to fade, and physical and emotional scars would still bear witness to their past. But with honesty and a shared commitment to Pippa, sensing Bruce's growing unease, he met his gaze with desperation. She knew that her past held secrets, shadows she had fought to keep hidden for far too long. But now, with the attack exposing their lives to danger, she understood that the time for secrets was over.

As Pippa took a deep breath, her voice trembled with vulnerability. She recounted her turbulent history, revealing a side of her life that Bruce had never fathomed. The words spilled forth, carrying darkness, violence, and the haunting pursuit of redemption. "I haven't always been the person you see before you, Bruce," Pippa started, her voice laden with regret and determination. "In my past, I was entangled with an underground organization that operated in society's darkest corners. It was a world fuelled by violence, deceit, and the pursuit of power."She spoke of her choices and the sacrifices she had endured. Pippa shared the horrors she had witnessed and the desperate search for redemption that had led her down this dangerous path. Her broken past pressed heavily upon her, leaving her vulnerable and exposed."I want you to know that I have fought to leave that life behind," Pippa continued, her voice quivering with raw emotion. "Every step I've taken with you has been a conscious effort to distance myself from the darkness that once consumed me. But the scars of my past are deep, haunting me still."Bruce listened intently, his heart heavy with the weight of Pippa's revelations. The truth she laid bare was a double-edged sword, cutting through his doubts and exposing her journey's immense complexity. He saw the pain etched in her eyes, and he couldn't deny the authenticity of her words. As Pippa spoke, Bruce's scars resonated with her story. He understood the struggle for redemption, the battle to distance oneself from a past defined by darkness. It was a shared journey, albeit through different paths. Silence settled between them, carrying the weight of their shared history. Bruce contemplated the impact of Pippa's revelations and the choices he now faced. The doubts that had once haunted him seemed to melt away, replaced by a newfound understanding of the complexities that shaped their bond. At that moment, Bruce made a choice. He embraced the imperfect, fragmented person before him, scars and all. He recognized that Pippa's past didn't define her present, just as his scars didn't define him. "Pippa," Bruce finally spoke, his voice filled with empathy and resolve. "I understand the dangerous path you have walked along. "But I also see the strength and resilience within you. We all have scars, some visible and others hidden deep within. What matters is who we are now and our choice moving forward." Pippa's eyes welled with tears, gratitude mingled with a touch of disbelief. She reached out, her trembling hand finding solace in Bruce's. "Thank you, Bruce," Pippa whispered, her voice choked with emotion. "Thank you for seeing me beyond my past, for allowing me to rewrite my story. Together, we can forge a future where our scars become symbols of strength and resilience."In that shared moment of understanding, Bruce and Pippa found solace in accepting each other's broken pasts. They knew their journey ahead would be fraught with challenges, but armed with newfound honesty and compassion, they were determined to face them together, rewriting their narrative of redemption. Silence settled between them, carrying the weight of their shared history. Bruce contemplated the impact of Pippa's revelations and the choices he now faced. The doubts that had once haunted him seemed to melt away, replaced by a newfound understanding of the complexities that shaped their bond. Through tearful conversations, painful introspection, and a willingness to listen, Bruce and Pippa slowly began to rebuild the bridge between them. Piece by piece, they faced the storm head-on, confronting the doubts threatening to tear them apart. As the storm subsided, a newfound clarity emerged. Bruce realized their scars were not just reminders of their pasts but testaments to their resilience. The journey to trust was not without its challenges, but in facing the doubts together, they had found a path forward. In the storm's aftermath, Bruce and Pippa emerged stronger, their bond tempered by the trials they had overcome. They understood that doubts would always be present but now had the tools to navigate them together. Their connection, once threatened, had weathered the storm, solidified their trust, and deepened their love. They began to devise a plan, a strategy to uncover the truth and expose those who sought to silence Pippa. Trust and open communication became their guiding principles as they shared their fears, doubts, and every piece of information they discovered. The darkness that had threatened to tear them apart now became the catalyst for their unwavering unity. As they embarked on their journey, the love they had found in each other became a beacon of hope, illuminating the path ahead. The shadows of the past might still linger, but together, they would face them, unafraid and determined.

In the face of adversity, Bruce and Pippa emerged as formidable forces ready to confront the darkness that had plagued them both. Their love became their shield, their trust a weapon against those who sought to extinguish the truth. In their unity, they found the strength to survive and uncover the secrets that threatened to tear their world apart.

# CHAPTER THREE

**B**ruce Logan's suspicions about Pippa had reached a crescendo, his mind consumed with the possibility of her involvement in the attack and her subsequent disappearance. Yet, as armed men descended upon them, the flames of suspicion were momentarily extinguished, replaced by the urgent need for survival. A wave of chilling recognition washed over Bruce and Pippa as they stared at the attackers, closing in on them. The resemblance was uncanny, a haunting reminder of the traumatic experience Bruce had endured in the past. The scars on his body throbbed with the weight of the memories, intertwining with the mounting tension in the air. The echoes of that fateful encounter resurfaced, amplifying the doubts and suspicions that had previously plagued their minds. Questions raced through Bruce's thoughts, threatening to unravel the fragile bond they had forged amidst the chaos. Could a deeper connection exist between the assailants and the dark forces that had targeted him before? Pippa, too, felt the weight of the moment. The echoes of the past seemed to mirror her shadowy history, casting a cloud of uncertainty over her intentions. The situation's intensity threatened to unravel the trust they had worked so hard to rebuild. Amid the encroaching danger, Bruce and Pippa found themselves at a crossroads. Would they succumb to the doubts and suspicions, allowing their fragile bond to crumble under the weight of the haunting similarities? Or would they summon the strength to confront their fears head-on, using their shared experiences as a driving force to overcome the looming darkness? Their gazes met, the turmoil reflected in their eyes. A shared understanding passed between them, the unspoken agreement that they would not let the echoes of the past consume them. The bond they had forged was not easily broken, and they had come too far to let doubt tear them apart. In a silent act of defiance, Bruce and Pippa took a step forward, and their determination reignited. They would face the assailants head-on, unravelling the mysteries that bound them together. The echoes of the past would no longer dictate their future. The tension in the air became a catalyst for their resilience. With each passing moment, their trust grew stronger, forged in the crucible of doubt and uncertainty. They channelled their shared strength, fighting for their survival and uncovering the truth that had brought them to this precipice. As the attackers closed in, Bruce and Pippa found solace in knowing they were not alone. They stood together, ready to confront the darkness that threatened to engulf them. In the face of the haunting echoes and the menacing presence before them, Bruce and Pippa found the resolve to press forward. They would face their assailants, unearthing the truth and protecting the fragile bond they had formed amidst the chaos. The echoes of their past would no longer haunt them; instead, they would serve as a reminder of their strength and the unbreakable trust that bound them together. As fear tightened its grip around Bruce's heart, a surge of vulnerability washed over him, intertwining with the painful throbbing of his scars. The weight of the danger they faced pressed upon him, igniting a frantic search to escape their difficult predicament. His mind raced, desperately seeking a glimmer of hope amidst the encroaching darkness. Surrounded and outnumbered, the odds seemed insurmountable. Bruce's instincts screamed at him to fight, to resist the impending threat. But deep down, a flicker of doubt danced within him, threatening to erode his resolve. Sensing Bruce's internal struggle, Pippa reached out a hand to gently touch his arm, grounding him in the present moment. Her eyes met his, conveying a mixture of determination and reassurance. Though the situation seemed dire, they were not alone in this fight. Drawing upon their shared strength, Bruce and Pippa locked eyes, finding solace in each other's presence. Their connection, though fragile, held the power to defy the odds stacked against them. They knew that succumbing to fear and doubt would only ensure their defeat. In a moment of clarity, Bruce's racing mind stilled. He focused on his breath, centering himself in the face of adversity. He recognized that true power lay not in the external circumstances but within their unwavering determination and resilience. With a deep breath, Bruce mustered the courage to confront the overwhelming odds. He refused to allow fear to dictate their fate. Instead, he embraced the vulnerability and transformed it into a driving force, a fuel that propelled him forward. Pippa, too, drew upon her wellspring of strength. She embraced her past, the shadows that had once haunted her, and channeled them into unwavering resolve. The scars on her own body became symbols of resilience and a reminder of the battles she had fought and survived. Side by side, Bruce and Pippa stood tall, ready to face whatever came their way. The odds may have been stacked against them, but they refused to be defined by mere statistics. They would defy expectations, pushing beyond their limits to protect what they held dear—their lives and the truth that had brought them together. Bruce and Pippa met the imminent threat with unwavering courage as the attackers closed in. They fought back, using their skills and resourcefulness to level the playing field. Their movements were synchronized, their determination unwavering. At that moment, surrounded by danger and uncertainty, Bruce and Pippa became a force to be reckoned with. The vulnerability that had threatened to consume them transformed into a wellspring of strength, propelling them forward. Though the outcome remained uncertain, Bruce and Pippa stood united, their bond unbreakable. They would face the storm together, refusing to let fear and doubt erode their resolve. In the face of overwhelming odds, they would fight with every fiber of their being, determined to overcome the darkness and emerge triumphant. Pippa's eyes flickered with determination and concern, her voice steady as she whispered, "Bruce, we can't let fear paralyze us. We have to rely on our instincts and each other to find a way out of this. We've faced danger before, and we'll do it again. Trust me."Her words struck a chord deep within Bruce, reigniting the flickering flame of courage that threatened to fade away. He locked eyes with Pippa, finding solace and strength in her unwavering conviction. With a nod, he acknowledged the trust they had built, the bond that had weathered storms before. In a moment of clarity, Bruce's racing mind stilled. He focused on his breath, cantering himself in the face of adversity. He recognized that the true power lay not in the external circumstances but within their unwavering determination and resilience. With a deep breath, Bruce mustered the courage to confront the overwhelming odds. He refused to allow fear to dictate their fate. Instead, he embraced the vulnerability and transformed it into a driving force, a fuel that propelled him forward. Pippa, too, drew upon her wellspring of strength. She embraced her past, the shadows that had once haunted her, and channeled them into unwavering resolve. The scars on her own body became symbols of resilience and a reminder of the battles she had fought and survived.

Side by side, Bruce and Pippa stood tall, ready to face whatever came their way. The odds may have been stacked against them, but they refused to be defined by mere statistics. They would defy expectations, pushing beyond their limits to protect what they held dear—their lives and the truth that had brought them together. At that moment, surrounded by danger and uncertainty, Bruce and Pippa became a force to be reckoned with. The vulnerability that had threatened to consume them transformed into a wellspring of strength, propelling them forward. Though the outcome remained uncertain, Bruce and Pippa stood united, their bond unbreakable. They would face the storm together, refusing to let fear and doubt erode their resolve. In the face of overwhelming odds, they would fight with every fiber of their being, determined to overcome the darkness and emerge triumphant. As Bruce and Pippa fought with calculated precision, their shared history became a wellspring of resilience, propelling them forward in the face of overwhelming odds. Their movements were swift and deliberate; each maneuver was a testament to their unyielding spirit and determination. Yet the stakes grew higher with each passing moment, and the danger escalated. The echoes of the past reverberated through Bruce's mind, reminding him of the darkness he had once confronted. The memories threatened to unravel his resolve, injecting doubt into his every move. Sensing Bruce's inner turmoil, Pippa recognized the weight of his past and the haunting echoes it carried. She bore her physical and emotional scars from the battles she had fought. She stepped closer to Bruce, her presence a silent reassurance, a reminder that they were in this together. Pippa's voice broke through the chaos in a rare lull between clashes. Her words were laced with a raw vulnerability, an acknowledgment of the ghosts that haunted them both. She spoke of the strength they had already summoned, the resilience that had carried them through their darkest moments. Bruce listened, his racing heart gradually steadying as he absorbed her words. He realized that memories need not dictate their present or future. The battles they had fought and the scars they bore were a testament to their survival.

With renewed determination, Bruce recentered himself into the present moment. He drew upon the strength that had propelled him through his darkest days, using it to fuel his every move. The echoes of the past no longer paralyzed him; they became a rallying cry, a reminder of his resilience.

As the confrontation raged on, Bruce and Pippa fought unwaveringly. They countered their attackers with strategic maneuvers, exploiting weaknesses and turning the tables whenever possible. Their movements were honed, their instincts razor-sharp.

The echoes of the past no longer haunted Bruce's every move; instead, they became a wellspring of strength and determination. With each clash, he drew upon his cultivated resilience, refusing to let doubt seep into his resolve. Together, they blazed through the chaos, defying the odds and the shadows that sought to shatter their spirits. Their shared bond, forged through adversity and tested in the crucible of uncertainty, propelled them forward with an unwavering sense of purpose. In their unity, Bruce and Pippa discovered a wellspring of resilience that no darkness could extinguish. They drew strength from each other, finding solace in their unspoken understanding. And with each step they took, they defied the looming shadows, carving their path towards a future where their shared strength and unwavering determination would prevail.

Bruce and Pippa discovered a moment of opportunity as the battle reached its crescendo.

With swift moves and calculated strategy, they gained the upper hand, turning the tide in their favor. The assailants, caught off guard, faltered in the face of their unwavering resolve. Finally, their attackers lay defeated, the tension in the air dissipating like a heavy fog. Bruce and Pippa stood amidst the aftermath, their bodies heaving with exertion but their spirits unbroken. They had faced the echoes of their past and emerged victorious. With a mix of relief and exhaustion, Bruce and Pippa locked eyes once more. The dangerous dance they had endured had tested them to their limits but also fortified their connection. They knew it was far from over, and more challenges awaited them, but they had faced the darkness together and emerged stronger. They took a moment to breathe, to gather their strength. The echoes of the past lingered, but their resolve burned bright. With renewed determination, Bruce and Pippa set their sights on the path ahead, ready to confront whatever awaited them, knowing that if they stood together, they could face any storm that came their way.

Just as they planned to exit, a new wave of attackers emerged from the corner, surrounding them like predator-surrounded prey. "We go again?" Bruce asked, his hand in a stance and his back touching Pippa's. "We go again," Pippa said, mentally picking who she would attack first. Their assailants moved with calculated precision, and their movements were coordinated and relentless. Drawing upon his SAS training, Bruce fought with every ounce of strength and skill. But the odds were stacked against him, and desperation gnawed at the edges of his resolve. As the skirmish raged on, a revelation unfolded before Bruce's eyes. Pippa's true character emerged with a magnetic intensity, shattering the doubts clouding his judgment. Her agility, resourcefulness, and unwavering determination surpassed his expectations, leaving him in awe. Bruce, in astonishment, caught side-eye glimpses as Pippa moved gracefully and precisely, her every action a testament to her hidden capabilities. She navigated the chaos with a confidence that belied her past struggles, evading attacks and countering with a swift and calculated prowess. Her skills complemented his own; their movements synchronized in an intricate survival dance. They fought side by side, their connection deepening with each shared moment of danger and triumph. Bruce's admiration for Pippa grew with each display of her skill, realizing she was not the fragile figure he had once imagined but a force to be reckoned with. Amid the skirmish, Pippa's strength of character shone brightly. She demonstrated a keen ability to adapt to ever-changing circumstances, utilizing her surroundings to gain an advantage. Her resourcefulness was a revelation to Bruce, dispelling any lingering doubts that had threatened their bond. As the battle raged on, Bruce couldn't help but feel a surge of pride for the woman who stood by his side. The doubts that had once plagued him now seemed insignificant in the face of Pippa's resilience and unwavering commitment. He saw her as a partner, an equal, and a formidable ally. At that moment, Bruce realized the depth of his feelings for Pippa. The love that had begun to blossom within him grew more robust, intertwined with a profound respect for the person she had become. The doubts that had once threatened to tear them apart faded into the background, overshadowed by the undeniable truth of Pippa's character. As the skirmish ended, the air was thick with exhaustion and triumph. Bruce and Pippa stood side by side, their bodies battered and their spirits emboldened. They locked eyes, their gazes filled with a newfound understanding and an unspoken acknowledgment they had discovered in each other. In the aftermath of that fight, Bruce's doubts had dissipated entirely as they caught their breath and surveyed the scene. Pippa had proven herself in the crucible of combat, revealing layers of courage and skill that surpassed his expectations. Their bond had been fortified, and he knew they could face any challenge. With a newfound sense of certainty, Bruce reached out, his hand finding hers. "Pippa, you amaze me. Your strength and resourcefulness are awe-inspiring. I no longer doubt you or the connection we share. Let's face whatever comes next, side by side." Pippa's eyes sparkled with gratitude and determination as she squeezed Bruce's hand. "Thank you, Bruce. Together, we are unstoppable. Whatever challenges we encounter, we will face them as a team, supporting and protecting each other." In that moment of unity, Bruce and Pippa embraced the truth of their bond. The doubts that once threatened to tear them apart had been transformed into a steadfast belief in their connection. With renewed strength and a shared purpose, they set their sights on the future, ready to face whatever trials awaited them, knowing their love and resilience would carry them through.As the adrenaline surged through his veins, Bruce's focus sharpened on the larger picture. The puzzle pieces started to align, revealing a sinister plot that extended far beyond their personal lives. Bruce's determination to uncover the truth burned brighter with every strike and parry. He fought for his survival and justice and the countless lives affected by the secrets lurking in the shadows. Realizing their attackers were pawns in a giant game granted his resolve to expose the web of deception and manipulation. Together, they moved deeper into the warehouse; the deeper they went, the more enemies they encountered. Beside him, Pippa fought with a fierce tenacity mirroring Bruce's unwavering determination. They moved as a well-coordinated team, each knowing the other's strengths and weaknesses. Their combined efforts became a testament to their shared commitment to the truth. Amidst the chaos, Bruce's mind raced, connecting the dots of Pippa's past, the attack, and the secrets that threatened to be buried. He understood that the very essence of their bond was rooted in their shared quest for truth and redemption. Doubts and suspicions now took a backseat as the bigger picture emerged. Bruce's voice cut through the din as they fought to an advantage. "Pippa, we can't let them silence us. We have to expose the truth, no matter the cost. We owe it to ourselves and those who have suffered under the weight of these secrets." Pippa's eyes burned with determination as she met Bruce's gaze. "You're right, Bruce. We can't back down. We'll fight until the truth is brought to light until justice is served." With a renewed sense of purpose, Bruce and Pippa pushed forward, their every move a testament to their unyielding resolve. They skillfully navigated the treacherous terrain, out-maneuvering their assailants with cunning strategy and unwavering determination. The battle went on a high crescendo, a tooth and nail fight, blows landing and body falling. Bruce, head bleeding with sweat, was face to face with one of the key figures behind the orchestrated attack. A man with a sinister smile, broken tooth, yellow teeth, and a knack for melee weapons held a bat in one hand and a nail remover in the other. He stood in parallel with Bruce. At that moment, he knew that the truth lay within reach. He confronted the figure with strength and conviction, demanding answers and exposing the intricate web of deceit. Bruce's doubts and suspicions shattered as the truth unfolded, replaced by a renewed clarity. The attack, the secrets, and Pippa's past were all part of a grand scheme to suppress the truth and maintain a façade of power and control. The puzzle pieces fell into place, revealing a darkness that had trapped them both. Pippa, dropping the last random man in the area, returns to Bruce's side and confronts the orchestrator, refusing to be silenced any longer. Their voices rang out, unearthing the buried truths and shining a light on the machinations that had kept them in the shadows. In a millisecond, they clashed. Blows connecting, jabs to the jaw, synchronized throw kicks, saliva, blood, and a piece of yellow tooth on the floor told the tale in the silent air. In the aftermath of the battle, as the dust settled and the truth prevailed, Bruce and Pippa stood as beacons of justice and resilience. They had fought not only for their survival but for the greater good. The doubts that once plagued their connection had been replaced by an unbreakable bond forged in the crucible of truth. With a renewed sense of purpose, Bruce and Pippa vowed to continue their journey, unearthing the remaining secrets and ensuring that those responsible faced the consequences of their actions. They knew the road ahead would be challenging, but their shared commitment to the truth would guide them through the darkness toward a future where the shadows held no power. Together, Bruce and Pippa would stand as a testament to the strength of the human spirit, refusing to let doubt or fear hinder their pursuit of justice. Their love, resilience, and unwavering determination would be a beacon of hope for all those seeking truth and redemption. Bruce and Pippa, bound by their shared experiences and unyielding loyalty, fought side by side with a synchronicity that surpassed mere physical coordination. Their connection went beyond words and gestures as an unspoken understanding and trust permeated their every move. Amid the intense battle, their palpable energy became a source of strength. Each strike they delivered, each dodge they executed, showcased their unwavering belief in each other's abilities. They moved as a well-oiled machine, seamlessly g each other's actions and supporting one another in the face of danger. The danger and uncertainty initially threatening to unravel their bond now catalyzed its strengthening. Every challenge they faced solidified their trust, as they relied on each other's skills and instincts to overcome seemingly insurmountable odds. Their unwavering trust formed an unbreakable bond, empowering them to push through exhaustion, fear, and doubt. They became a formidable duo, their collective presence radiating a sense of determination and resilience that inspired those around them. With the yellow-gender man defeated, it released a wave of more thugs. It now felt like a level in a game to Bruce. Whether they came for revenge or wanted to trample on them like chicken on feeds. Bruce and Pippa stood back to back in the dimly lit, abandoned warehouse, their breaths heavy and hearts pounding as the menacing thugs encircled them. The air was tense, and their breath was the only sound. The flickering, pale light from a lone, cracked window revealed the dust-covered, broken furniture and scattered debris strewn across the concrete floor. With a determined glint in their eyes, Bruce and Pippa prepared for the inevitable confrontation. At the speed of light, Bruce reached for a rusty metal pipe while Pippa picked up a discarded wooden plank. Their faces conveyed a mix of anxiety and determination. The thugs lunged forward, and the fight erupted in motion. Bruce's pipe and Pippa's plank became an extension of themselves. They moved with fluidity, almost dancing amidst the chaos. Bruce's strikes were precise and powerful, while Pippa's agility allowed her to evade the thugs' attacks, swiftly countering with her wooden weapon. With each swing of their makeshift weapons, they shattered wooden crates, sending splinters flying. The dusty air became thick with the acrid scent of sweat and fear. The thugs, initially overconfident, began to falter under the relentless assault from the determined duo. Bruce's pipe landed with a resounding thud against a thug's arm, eliciting a howl of pain. Pippa's plank smacked into another's shins, sending him tumbling to the ground. The warehouse became a battlefield, with broken furniture and debris scattered across the floor, now serving as both a challenge and an advantage. The duo somersaulted off crates, used a wooden board as a makeshift shield, and swung from the rafters to gain a strategic vantage point. They turned their surroundings into their ally, every move calculated and precise. Now and then, the duo would exchange their weapons with elite precision during exchange. The remaining thugs circled Bruce and Pippa, their bravado replaced by desperation. In a final display of teamwork, Bruce and Pippa used their surroundings to their advantage. Bruce kicked a pile of rocks towards their assailants, causing a temporary distraction, while Pippa leaped onto a stack of crates, launching herself off with a flying kick right on the jaw that sent the last thug crashing into a pile of splintered wood. Bruce and Pippa stood victorious but exhausted, with the warehouse now eerily silent. They leaned on each other for support, their backs pressed together, as the adrenaline began to subside. Their hearts pounded in unison, and they shared a triumphant smile, their eyes filled with a sense of accomplishment and a deep connection.

But just as they thought the battle was over, a new group of thugs appeared at the entrance, a glint of malice in their eyes. "Is there like a queen that lays thug eggs every damn second?" Bruce said under his breath. "This is their nest, dimwit," Pippa replied. "When does it end?" "It doesn't. Now, let's kick-ass," They charged and clashed.

As the chaos of the battle reached its crescendo, Bruce's sharp instincts detected a fleeting opportunity for escape. Without hesitation, he locked eyes with Pippa, their unspoken understanding fuelling their coordinated plan.

In a synchronized movement, Bruce and Pippa unleashed a torrent of strikes and maneuvers, their skill and precision creating a diversion that left their attackers momentarily stunned. Exploiting the confusion, they swiftly disengaged from the confrontation, slipping away into the cover of darkness. The night became their ally as they embraced its cloak, their footsteps muffled against the pavement as they navigated the labyrinthine streets. Bruce and Pippa moved with a calculated urgency, their hearts pounding in unison with the rhythm of their escape. Silent communication passed between them, each anticipating the other's next move. They weaved through alleyways, blending seamlessly with the shadows, leaving their bewildered assailants in their wake. The echoes of their pursuers' frustration resonated through the night air as they realized their prey had eluded their grasp. Breathing a momentary sigh of relief, Bruce and Pippa found a secluded spot where they could briefly rest and regroup. Adrenaline still coursed through their veins, but a renewed sense of determination burned within them. They knew their escape was just the beginning, a respite to gather their thoughts to plan their next move. In the quiet darkness, Bruce and

Pippa exchanged a knowing glance, their eyes reflecting a shared understanding of the journey ahead. The doubts that once threatened to tear them apart were replaced with an unwavering belief in their abilities and the bond they had forged. "We made it," Bruce said, his voice calm but filled with triumph. "We slipped through their fingers, Pippa."

Pippa nodded, a mix of relief and determination shining in her eyes. "But we can't let our guard down. They won't stop pursuing us until their secrets are safe. We must continue, Bruce. We have to find the truth." Bruce nodded in agreement, his gaze fixed on Pippa's face. "We will, Pippa. Together, we'll uncover the truth and bring those responsible to justice. Our escape was just the first step. We'll stay one step ahead, guided by our trust in each other." Bruce and Pippa's resolve solidified amidst

the shadows and uncertainty. The doubts that once threatened their bond were replaced by an unyielding determination to unravel the secrets that had brought them to this point. They knew that the road ahead would be treacherous. Still, they were prepared to face it together, drawing strength from their shared escape, but they were prepared to face it together, drawing strength from their shared escape and unbreakable trust. As they disappeared into the night, their steps guided by an unwavering belief in each other, Bruce and Pippa became more than mere individuals. They became a formidable force, a beacon of resilience and determination, committed to exposing the truth and reclaiming their lives from the clutches of darkness. In the dimly lit hideout, Bruce and Pippa caught their breath, the echoes of the battle still reverberating in their minds. The weight of the near-death experience hung heavy in the air, reminding them of the fragility of their existence. As they regained their composure, a renewed determination settled within them both. The adrenaline that had fuelled their fight now transformed into a steadfast resolve. They knew they couldn't afford to dwell on the close call; instead, they needed to channel their energy into their mission to uncover the truth and expose those responsible. Sitting side by side, Bruce and Pippa shared a moment of silent understanding. Their eyes met, and in that exchange, they reaffirmed their commitment to each other and the cause that had brought them together. "We can't let fear or doubt consume us," Bruce said, his voice filled with determination and urgency. "What we've just been through only strengthens our resolve. We have to push forward, Pippa. We owe it to ourselves and all those who have suffered under the weight of these secrets. Pippa nodded, her expression resolute. "You're right, Bruce. We can't afford to waver now. This fight is bigger than us. We can make a difference, expose the truth, and bring justice to those who deserve it. We won't let them intimidate or deter us from our path. "As they spoke, the fragments of doubt that had once plagued their minds began to dissolve. The chaos they had endured had sharpened their focus, reminding them of the urgency and importance of their mission. Amid the aftermath, Bruce and Pippa formed a pact—a silent vow to face whatever challenges awaited them with unwavering determination. They knew the road ahead would be perilous, fraught with danger and uncertainties, but they were prepared to navigate it together.Bruce and Pippa rose from their temporary refuge with a shared purpose, their minds now clear and their hearts aligned. The scars they bore, both physical and emotional, became badges of resilience, driving them forward in their quest for truth and justice."Go home and stay safe. I'll let you know what you must do, okay?" Bruce stopped in his tracks and looked at Pippa."Sure. Be safe, please. And I'm sorry." Pippa looked at him. Bruce knew Pippa had his soft spot. He nodded, then smiled and watched her disappear into the darkness.As they ventured back into the shadows, ready to confront the unknown, their steps were guided by a renewed fire within. The doubts that had once threatened their bond were replaced by an unbreakable trust and a shared conviction that they were meant to face this journey together.The battle they had just survived had transformed them, strengthening their resolve and fortifying their connection. Bruce and Pippa were now prepared to face whatever lay ahead, united by their shared purpose and unyielding determination. The aftermath of the terrifying attack had become the catalyst for their transformation, propelling them into a future where the truth would be uncovered and justice would prevail. Bruce and Pippa now stood even more united. Their shared cause superseded any lingering doubts or suspicions. The shattered remnants of their past uncertainties were replaced by an unyielding belief in each other and their mission.With newfound clarity, they understood their bond was stronger than the shadows that threatened to tear them apart. They had both been tested individually and together and emerged stronger for it. The trust they had rekindled amidst the chaos was now an unbreakable force guiding them forward.They knew the path ahead would be treacherous, lined with obstacles and hidden dangers. The forces that sought to destroy them were powerful, but they were fuelled by a collective determination that transcended their doubts.Hand in hand, Bruce and Pippa pledged to protect the fragile connection they had forged. They would be each other's anchors, supporting and encouraging one another in moments of doubt. They recognized that their shared journey was about seeking the truth and preserving the bond they had nurtured amidst the chaos.Their investigation would lead them deeper into the web of secrets, challenging their resolve and testing their trust. But they faced the challenges with unwavering determination, knowing their united front was their greatest strength. Together, they would unveil the truth, exposing the forces that lurked in the shadows. They would fight for justice, not just for themselves but for all those who had suffered under the weight of deception and manipulation. As they embarked on this dangerous path, they carried the lessons learned from the aftermath of the terrifying attack. Their doubts had been shattered, replaced by a steadfast belief in each other and the cause they shared. They would not allow anything to come between them, for their bond was fortified by the trials they had overcome.In the face of adversity, Bruce and Pippa would stand shoulder to shoulder, their connection unbreakable. With unwavering trust and a shared commitment to the truth, they would navigate the intricate maze of lies and deceit, emerging victorious on the other side.The aftermath of the terrifying attack had changed them, molding them into warriors of justice. Their suspicion of one another had been shattered, replaced by a profound understanding of their shared purpose. Together, they would face the unknown, uncover the truth, and protect the fragile connection they had forged amidst the chaos.Bruce and Pippa set forth on a new path, their resolve strengthened by the crucible of adversity. The attackers had failed to break their spirit, igniting a flame that burned brighter than ever before. Their journey had taken an unexpected turn, propelling them deeper into a web of intrigue and danger. Still, they were ready to face whatever challenges lay ahead, united against the common enemy that threatened their existence. Having escaped the clutches of the mysterious thugs, Bruce knew he had to act swiftly to uncover the identity of their assailants and why they were targeted. He reached for his phone and sent a text message to Pippa."Stay low, Pippa. I need to find out who's behind this. It's not safe for you right now. Trust me. I'll be in touch."Pippa acknowledged the message with a nod. She dropped her phone, and Bruce went to a nearby café, maintaining a low profile. He ordered a coffee and a sandwich, eating in silence. The other patrons greeted him, but he responded with polite nods and nothing more. His mind was preoccupied with the looming questions and threats that surrounded them. After finishing his meal, Bruce hailed a cab and headed to Detective Christopher Hunter's house. He knew that if anyone could help him unravel this mystery, it was his old friend. As he entered the detective's home, Christopher's wife, Ava, welcomed him warmly."Good to see you, Bruce. Chris is in the bedroom, getting dressed. I'll let him know you're here."Bruce nodded in gratitude and waited as

Christopher emerged from the bedroom, buttoning up his shirt."Hey, Bruce. What brings you here?" Christopher asked, a hint of curiosity in his voice.Bruce's expression grew serious as he ushered Christopher to a quieter corner of the room. "Chris, it's not what it seems. I need your help, and I can't explain everything here. It's more than just a gang brawl. I was involved, and I'm in over my head."Detective Hunter's brow furrowed in concern. "Bruce, I've got a report of gang brawls at an abandoned warehouse that I need to check out. What's going on?"

Bruce leaned in closer, his voice low and urgent. "Chris, this isn't your typical gang. They're professionals, and they're after me. I must return to that warehouse, but I can't do it alone. I need your help to access the crime scene and find any possible clues. Please, Chris, I can't do this without you."Christopher Hunter, after a moment of contemplation, sighed and nodded. "All right, Bruce. I can't turn my back on an old friend. Let's go to the warehouse together."Bruce's relief was palpable. He knew that with Christopher's assistance, they had a better chance of uncovering the truth behind the relentless attacks. The two friends left the house, got into Christopher's car, and drove towards the abandoned warehouse. In the aftermath and thoughts of the harrowing encounter with their assailants in this same warehouse, Bruce Logan stood amidst the debris, his mind grappling with the identity and motives of those who had attacked them. The need for answers grew urgent, and it was at that moment that a familiar face emerged from the shadows.Homicide Detective Christopher Hunter, a trusted friend and ally, stepped onto the scene. Christopher and Bruce had shared a bond forged in the crucible of their time in the Army together. Christopher's decision to join the County of Essex Police Department after their service had led him down a different path, but their friendship remained steadfast.As Christopher surveyed the scene, his sharp gaze took in the damage and the signs of the unfolding struggle. He recognized the situation's gravity and the danger lurking in the shadows. With a nod of acknowledgment to Bruce, he approached, ready to offer his support and expertise.A sense of relief washed over Bruce. He knew that Christopher's experience as a detective would be instrumental in unraveling the tangled web of motives and connections that had entangled their lives.With a firm resolve,

Christopher set to work, meticulously examining the evidence left behind by the assailants. He pieced together the fragments, drawing connections and formulating theories as he delved deeper into the investigation. His instincts honed by years of police work, Christopher was determined to uncover the truth.Bruce and Christopher formed a formidable team as they shared information and insights. The camaraderie that had defined their time in the Army was reignited, fuelling their pursuit of justice and the search for answers. Together, they navigated the treacherous landscape of deceit and danger, determined to expose the hidden forces threatening their lives.Christopher also offered Bruce a much-needed perspective and grounding influence during their collaboration. He served as a voice of reason, challenging Bruce's preconceived notions and reminding him of the importance of trust and loyalty.Bruce and Christopher stood side by side, ready to face the challenges ahead. With Christopher's expertise and unwavering support, they were poised to bring the truth to light and confront the adversaries who sought to tear their world apart. Their bond, forged in the crucible of their shared experiences, would be tested once again as they embarked on a perilous journey that would push their skills and determination to the limit.The discovery of a name connected to the DNA samples found at the scene of the attack ignited a glimmer of hope for Bruce Logan and Detective Christopher Hunter.Leonard Austin Frost, a lumberman residing in one of the lowly suburbs of the town, emerged as a potential key to unraveling the mystery that had plagued their lives.With renewed determination, Bruce and Christopher began investigating Leonard Austin Frost, recognizing that he held the answers they desperately sought. They delved into the life of the enigmatic lumberman, digging deep into his background and connections.Their inquiries led them to the outskirts of the town, where the lowly suburbs hid a dark underbelly. The streets were lined with dilapidated houses, and an air of desolation clung to the atmosphere. Leonard's residence stood as a lone structure, seemingly blending into the backdrop of neglect and forgotten dreams.As they approached the residence, anticipation mingled with caution. Knowing they were closing in on a potential perpetrator filled the air with electric tension. With each step closer to the truth, Bruce and

Christopher braced themselves for the confrontation.Inside the modest dwelling, they found themselves face-to-face with Leonard Austin Frost, a weathered man with a haunted gaze. The lines etched into his face told tales of a troubled past, and as Bruce and Christopher pressed him for answers, they could sense the weight of his secrets.Leonard's story unfolded like a tapestry of pain and desperation. He revealed his involvement with a clandestine organization that operated in the shadows, manipulating lives and orchestrating chaos. His narrative threads wove a web that ensnared not only Bruce and Pippa but countless others who unknowingly became pawns in a giant game. As Leonard Austin Frost spoke, the puzzle pieces began to fit together. The trial led to influential figures with vested interests willing to go to any lengths to protect their secrets. In the presence of Leonard, Bruce, and Christopher faced a choice: succumb to fear and uncertainty or rise above and fight for justice. With unwavering resolve, they decided to bring down the corrupt forces orchestrating their torment.

Bruce and Christopher emerged from Leonard's residence, their determination etched into their expressions. Armed with newfound knowledge, they embarked on a mission to test their mettle and push them to their limits. The final battle against the shadowy organization loomed on the horizon, and they would stop at nothing to expose the truth and protect those they held dear.

# CHAPTER FOUR

**3 DAYS EARLIER.**

Bruce was troubled. He had to do something about Pippa. Who was this woman he was in love with? To do that, he had no choice but to delve deeper into Pippa's past. His quest for the truth pushed him to commit a grand larceny act he never considered. Driven by a desperate need to uncover Pippa's secrets, he rummaged through her apartment, searching for evidence to shed light on her identity. As Bruce sifted through Pippa's personal belongings, guilt began to gnaw at his conscience. He recognized that he was invading her privacy, delving into the depths of her past without her knowledge or consent. The weight of his actions settled heavily on his shoulders, casting a shadow over his thoughts. The puzzle pieces of Jennifer Alvarez's life formed a complex tapestry with each document and memo he uncovered. Bruce's curiosity clashed with his guilt as he grappled with the moral dilemma of invading Pippa's privacy. He questioned whether his actions were justified in uncovering the truth or if he was succumbing to his doubts and suspicions. The memos held stories and memories, each adding another layer of complexity to the person he thought he knew. Bruce felt curiosity, concern, and a growing desire to understand the truth hidden within Pippa's past. But with each item he examined, the guilt intensified.

In that moment of conflict, Bruce realized that the weight of guilt was a reminder of his humanity, of the consequences of his actions. He knew he had to tread carefully, balancing his need for the truth with respect for Pippa's boundaries. Setting aside the belongings he had uncovered, Bruce made a decision. He would confront Pippa, not with accusations or judgment, but with vulnerability and honesty. He would share his doubts and suspicions, expressing the internal struggle he had been wrestling with. He would allow her to reveal the truth on her terms and share her side of the story without invading her privacy. Bruce understood that trust was a delicate thread, easily frayed by doubt and violation. It was only through open communication and mutual respect that they could navigate the challenges that lay ahead. He resolved to apologize for his intrusion, acknowledging the weight of his actions and the impact they had on their relationship. With a heavy heart, Bruce closed the box containing Pippa's belongings. He carried it with him, a physical reminder of his crossed line and the need for redemption. He sought a chance to make amends and rebuild the trust his actions had shaken. In the face of guilt and uncertainty, Bruce and Pippa stood at a crossroads. At that moment, they would be tested, and their bond challenged. They chose whether to let guilt and doubt tear them apart or to confront the shadows together, weaving their connection with newfound strength and understanding. With each revelation, Bruce grew increasingly conflicted.

The name "Jennifer Alvarez" resonated within him, a reminder of the woman he had come to care for deeply. Yet, her deliberate concealment of her identity, even her Spanish heritage, left him with a sense of betrayal and unease. The passport, college documents, and other items Bruce discovered painted a picture of a complex and carefully crafted facade. Jennifer Alvarez had kept her past shrouded in secrecy, her true self hidden behind an impenetrable mask. Not even her accent, a tell-tale sign for most, had given a clue to her Spanish origins.

The weight of the truth bore down upon Bruce, who realized his actions' significance. Confronting Pippa with what he had discovered would undoubtedly fracture their fragile trust, irreparably damaging the bond they had forged. The knowledge he now possessed could not be undone, but he had a choice—whether to confront her or continue down the path of uncertainty. Bruce grappled with the consequences of his actions. The truth he had uncovered about Jennifer Alvarez, Pippa's hidden past and identity, remained a closely guarded secret. The revelation had only deepened the mystery surrounding her motives and the web of deception in which they were entangled. As their journey continued, Bruce vowed to protect Pippa.

**PRESENT DAY**

After parting with Detective Christopher, Bruce's quest for more answers unexpectedly turned when he witnessed a dangerous encounter between Pippa and a mysterious woman named Elaine Murphy. The puzzle pieces rearranged as he watched the altercation unfold, revealing deeper intrigue and danger. He followed her after that, traversing through street after street, alleyway after alleyway until he found himself inside a club.

He sat at a bar, watching her every move while engaging a woman who had picked an interest in him. "Holding a convo like you hold your liquor, I like that," she flattered.

"Every moment is an occasion," he smiled, eyes scanning the room. He followed when he saw Elaine leave her seat and into the convenience. In the dimly lit club restroom, Bruce and Elaine engaged in a desperate struggle, their bodies colliding with the urgency of a life-or-death situation. Blow after blow, they fought with a ferocity fuelled by their respective agendas. But amidst the chaos, a crucial revelation emerged. Through gritted teeth and amidst labored breaths, Elaine Murphy disclosed a shocking truth—Pippa, or Jennifer Alvarez, was an undercover officer from the Montebello Police Department. She had infiltrated a powerful drug ring, and her mission led her to the County of Essex. The conspiracy she was investigating threatened Bruce and countless others whose lives hung in the balance. As Bruce absorbed this revelation, the gravity of the situation began to weigh heavily upon him. The complexities of Pippa's hidden identity, her involvement in a dangerous undercover operation, and the implications of the conspiracy entangled in a web of deception stretched far beyond what he had imagined. With Elaine's disclosure, Bruce had a choice—to trust Pippa's true intentions and align himself with her in the fight against the drug ring or to distance himself from the danger threatening to consume them both. Though uncertainty lingered, Bruce recognized the bravery and sacrifice Pippa had made by going undercover, risking her safety to expose the truth. He understood that their paths had converged not by chance but by a twist of fate, intertwining their lives in a way neither could have anticipated. Bruce, Elaine, and Pippa were at a crossroads, their fates entwined in a dangerous game of cat and mouse. The revelation of Pippa's true identity and her role as an undercover officer illuminated the stakes of their mission. Knowing that they were up against a powerful drug ring and a far-reaching conspiracy, they prepared to face the challenges ahead, united in their pursuit of justice and the truth. Bruce, now his back on the wall, staring at the floor with water dancing around, a broken toilet sink, and a piece of his collar, looked at Elaine, who was also resting on the toilet seat. "Look, I'm sorry. I'm just trying to protect the woman I love," It's all right. I've been in worse. I understand. "Bruce rearranged his clothes and left the restroom. The bouncer who stood there smiled at him. "Heard some noises.

You are one of a kind the way you do your thing," Bruce smiled and nodded. He walked towards the bar and dropped a couple of dollars on the counter for the drink he and the woman earlier drank."And where have you been?" She asked him.

"Just getting shit done," Bruce smiled and turned to leave.

"At least a number would do?" She called him back. "I'm taken," he replied under the booming sound of the music without turning around and exiting the club.

# CHAPTER FIVE

As the cracks in their relationship deepened, Bruce and Pippa found themselves at odds. The weight of their differing perspectives and approaches to the unfolding case strained the fragile bond they had forged amidst the chaos. The once-solid foundation of trust now trembled under their conflicting viewpoints.

Bruce believed in pushing forward aggressively, driven by his need for answers and justice. He was determined to uncover the truth at any cost, even if it meant taking risks and disregarding their safety. For him, the situation's urgency demanded swift action and unwavering determination.

On the other hand, Pippa, conscious of the dangers that lurked in the shadows, urged caution and strategic planning. She understood the gravity of the situation and the need to protect themselves from the powerful forces they were up against. Her perspective was rooted in self- preservation and ensuring they had a calculated approach to the unfolding events. Their differing viewpoints clashed, creating a growing divide between them. Each held firm to their beliefs, unable to find common ground amidst the mounting tension.The wedge driven between them widened with each disagreement, threatening to shatter the fragile bond they had once cherished. Communication became strained, laden with unspoken frustrations and misunderstandings. Their conversations grew heated, filled with accusations and defensiveness. The trust they had built slowly eroded, replaced by doubt and skepticism. Amid the turmoil, Bruce and Pippa found themselves questioning the very foundation of their connection. The doubts that had plagued Bruce from the beginning resurfaced, fuelling his suspicion. He wondered if Pippa's caution was born out of a hidden agenda and if she was withholding crucial information that could alter the course of their investigation.

Pippa felt betrayed by Bruce's accusations and lack of trust. She had opened up to him, revealing her turbulent past, yet he seemed to doubt her intentions. She questioned whether their bond was strong enough to withstand the strain of their differing perspectives and the secrets that still lingered in the shadows.

As danger loomed and the case unraveled, the tension between Bruce and Pippa reached its breaking point. They were faced with a choice — to either find a way to bridge the divide and rediscover their shared purpose or to let their relationship crumble under the weight of their conflicting viewpoints.

In the face of this pivotal moment, Bruce and Pippa needed to confront their doubts and fears head-on. They needed an open and honest dialogue to listen to each other's perspectives without judgment. They needed to find a compromise that would allow them to proceed together, their strengths complementing each other rather than tearing them apart.

The road ahead was uncertain and fraught with challenges and dangers. But Bruce and Pippa had to remember the bond they had once shared, the connection that had drawn them together in the first place. They needed to find common ground to rebuild trust and understanding.

As they stood at the crossroads, Bruce and Pippa faced a defining moment. It was up to them to decide whether their relationship would crumble under the weight of their differences or whether they would find a way to bridge the divide and emerge stronger, united in their shared purpose. The choice they made would shape not only their investigation but also the future of their connection.

As the danger escalated and the case grew more perilous, Pippa's concerns shifted toward their safety. She believed that involving Bruce in the investigation only heightened their risks. In her perspective, the police department possessed the necessary resources and expertise to handle the situation without putting themselves in harm's way.

Pippa's primary focus was on the immediate danger that surrounded them. She worried about the potential consequences of their continued involvement, fearing that they would become even more wanted than mere targets. In her eyes, stepping back and allowing the authorities to take over seemed like the most prudent course of action.

This perspective overshadowed the bigger picture for Pippa. She was primarily concerned with their well-being and the preservation of their lives. The dangers they encountered made her question whether their pursuit of the truth was worth their risks. For her, protecting themselves took precedence over unearthing the full extent of the case.

On the other hand, Bruce remained driven by his need for justice and closure. He believed that their involvement was crucial in unraveling the truth and bringing those responsible to account. While acknowledging the dangers, he was willing to take calculated risks to achieve their shared goal.

The differing perspectives created a significant divide between Bruce and Pippa. Bruce saw the case as a chance to make a difference, to uncover the truth that had eluded others. He believed their unique insights and tenacity gave them an advantage over the police, whose resources might be stretched thin.

However, Pippa's concerns for their safety and the potential consequences of their actions weighed heavily on her. She was not willing to jeopardize their lives for the sake of justice. The immediate danger became her primary focus, clouding her judgment regarding the bigger picture.

The tension between Bruce and Pippa intensified as their viewpoints clashed. They struggled to find common ground, with each clinging stubbornly to their convictions. The lack of consensus threatened to fracture their bond as doubts and frustrations festered beneath the surface.

In the face of these conflicting perspectives, Bruce and Pippa needed to find a way to bridge the gap between them. They had to recognize and respect each other's concerns while also considering the broader implications of their actions. It required open communication, compromise, and a commitment to their purpose.

Bruce's unwavering determination to uncover the truth and bring the culprits to justice remained unwavering. He couldn't shake off the nagging feeling that the events unfolding were somehow connected to him. The weight of responsibility settled heavily on his shoulders, fuelling his unwavering principles and urging him to confront the evil that lurked in the shadows.

For Bruce, it was not just about solving the case; it was about personal redemption and finding closure for the past traumas that haunted him. He believed his involvement was vital in untangling the intricate web of deceit and unearthing the truth that had eluded others.

The notion that the crimes could be connected to him only intensified his resolve. He couldn't ignore the possibility that his past actions had attracted the attention of dangerous individuals, and now it was his duty to face the consequences head-on.

While Pippa's concerns for their safety were valid, Bruce saw himself as a catalyst in the events that had transpired. He believed that stepping back would not only be a betrayal to himself but also a missed opportunity to right the wrongs that had been done. He couldn't allow fear to dictate his actions or inhibit the pursuit of justice.

Bruce's unwavering principles and determination to confront evil head-on created further tension between him and Pippa. She struggled to reconcile his steadfast commitment with her concerns for their safety. The divide between their viewpoints widened, threatening to fracture their bond.

Finding common ground and aligning their goals became crucial in navigating the challenges ahead. It would require compromise, trust, and a shared understanding of the risks. Bruce would need to address Pippa's concerns and work together to develop a strategy that balanced their pursuit of the truth while ensuring their well-being.

Pippa listened intently as Bruce shared his concerns and convictions. She could sense the situation's weight and understood their involvement's gravity. The tension in their relationship had been palpable, but Bruce's words resonated with her.

"I hear you, Bruce," Pippa replied, her voice filled with empathy and determination. "I know this journey we're on is not without its challenges, and it has taken a toll on us. But you're right. Our pursuit of truth and justice is bigger than ourselves. We are responsible for doing what we can to prevent further harm."

She paused for a moment, collecting her thoughts. "I won't deny that I'm scared, Bruce. The risks are real, and it's unsettling to think about what might happen if we walk away. But we've come this far, and we've already seen the impact of our actions. Our involvement has saved lives, and I can't ignore that."

Pippa took a deep breath, her eyes meeting Bruce's. "If we let fear guide our decisions and let the uncertainty consume us, then we've already lost. We owe it to ourselves and those who have suffered to stay involved. We can't disregard the potential consequences of inaction. Together, I believe we can make a difference, and maybe, just maybe, we can bring about the truth and justice we seek."

Bruce nodded, appreciating Pippa's understanding and resilience. He realized that their shared commitment to the cause had drawn them together in the first place. Despite the strain, they were united in pursuing the greater good.

"You're right, Pippa," Bruce said, his voice filled with determination. "Our convictions and the lives at stake outweigh our challenges. Let's stay involved, face the risks together, and do everything possible to end this darkness. We owe it to ourselves and the victims."

Bruce continued, his voice earnest and determined. "The attacks we've been investigating are becoming more frequent and vicious. Lives are at stake, and we can't afford to let personal considerations overshadow our pursuit of justice. I need your insight and expertise to help me understand the patterns, motives, and possible culprits behind these crimes."

Pippa's gaze met Bruce's, a mixture of wariness and lingering resentment evident in her eyes. She hesitated for a moment, grappling with her own conflicting emotions. Ultimately, she recognized the importance of their partnership and the need to work together.

"I understand, Bruce," she finally replied, her voice tinged with vulnerability and determination. "Despite our differences, our shared commitment to justice brought us together. I may have reservations, but I also acknowledge the importance of pooling our resources and knowledge to solve these crimes."

Bruce's heart lifted slightly at Pippa's response. He sensed an opportunity to gather crucial information without disclosing his discoveries or further straining their relationship.

I appreciate your willingness to put our differences aside," Bruce said, his voice filled with gratitude. "Now, based on what we've learned so far, what are your thoughts on the motives and potential connections behind these attacks? Are there any leads we can pursue?"

Pippa's gaze shifted, her mind racing with the knowledge she held, but she refrained from revealing everything. She knew there were limits to what she could share, especially with their lingering mistrust.

"I have some working theories, Bruce," she responded carefully. "But we must be cautious and gather more evidence before jumping to conclusions. The attacks seem calculated and orchestrated, indicating a level of organization we haven't fully grasped. There could be hidden forces at play, individuals with their agendas."

Bruce nodded, appreciating Pippa's cautious approach. "I understand, Pippa. Let's proceed with care and continue to piece together the puzzle. We'll need to gather more information, follow any leads, and work together to uncover the truth."

Bruce and Pippa knew their next steps were crucial as they navigated the delicate balance between their dynamics and shared commitment. The tension remained, but a glimmer of hope sparked within them—the hope of bringing justice to the victims and finding a way to reconcile their differences.

Bruce's calm demeanor betrayed the lingering turmoil within him. He chose his words carefully, trying to maintain composure as he addressed Pippa. Sensing an opportunity to gather more information, he focused on her apparent knowledge of the recent attacks.

"Pippa, I couldn't help but notice that you seem to be following the news closely," Bruce began, his voice steady. "Do you happen to know anything more about the recent attacks? Any additional details or insights that could help us in our investigation?"

Pippa hesitated for a moment, her gaze shifting slightly. She weighed her options, contemplating how much to reveal without compromising her sources or further exacerbating the strained atmosphere between them.

"I... I've been doing some independent research," Pippa finally admitted, her voice tinged with caution. "There have been whispers, unverified reports that suggest a possible connection between the attacks. Some patterns are emerging, but drawing concrete conclusions is still early."

Bruce nodded; his curiosity intensified. "What kind of patterns are you seeing?"

Pippa took a deep breath, choosing her words carefully. "There are similarities in the modus operandi and the choice of targets. The perpetrators appear to be deliberate in their selection, targeting individuals with specific connections or backgrounds. There's a possibility of a hidden agenda, a motive beyond random acts of violence."

Bruce's mind raced, piecing together the information he had learned and the insights Pippa shared. It seemed like they were beginning to unravel a tangled web of darkness and secrets.

"Have you encountered any names or possible suspects in your research?" Bruce asked, his voice filled with a mix of anticipation and caution.

Pippa hesitated once more, her gaze flickering before meeting Bruce's eyes. "I can't disclose everything just yet, Bruce. The information I've gathered is incomplete, and I'm still working to corroborate it. But I believe we're dealing with a sophisticated and well-connected group. There could be powerful individuals involved, hidden behind layers of secrecy."

Bruce absorbed Pippa's words, feeling a mixture of frustration and intrigue. He recognized the importance of cautiously proceeding as the stakes grew higher with every revelation.

"Thank you, Pippa, for sharing what you can," Bruce said, his voice filled with gratitude. "Let's continue to piece together the puzzle. We must gather more evidence, follow any leads, and uncover the truth behind these attacks. Our commitment to justice remains steadfast, even amidst our challenges."

Pippa nodded in agreement, a renewed sense of determination in her eyes. Despite the lingering tension between them, they both understood the significance of their partnership and the shared pursuit of truth. Together, they would navigate the murky waters, uncover the hidden connections, and shed light on the darkness that plagued their investigation.

Bruce's brows furrowed in confusion as he watched Pippa abruptly dash out of the apartment, leaving him puzzled and curious about the sudden departure. Right after their conversation, the timing of her exit left him questioning her motives and intentions. Uncertainty filled the air, and Bruce couldn't help but wonder if Pippa's swift exit was related to their discussion or was driven by something entirely unrelated. Guilt, fear, or other unknown factors raced through Bruce's mind as he tried to make sense of the situation. He considered following her, but a part of him recognized the need to respect her space and give her time to process whatever might have triggered her sudden departure. As he stood there, Bruce pondered the possibilities. Perhaps the weight of the conversation had overwhelmed Pippa, and she needed a moment alone to collect her thoughts. It was also plausible that her exit was prompted by fear, triggered by the mention of dangerous individuals or the realization that they were delving into a dangerous web of corruption. However, Bruce couldn't ignore the nagging thought that there might be another reason for Pippa's sudden departure. Was there something else at play, something entirely unrelated to their conversation? Could she have received a distressing message or encountered an unexpected obstacle? With a mix of curiosity and concern, Bruce decided to give Pippa time to gather herself, hoping that she would eventually return or explain her abrupt exit. In the meantime, he resolved to use the moment of solitude to reflect on their shared conversation and further contemplate his discoveries. Bruce's mind buzzed with unanswered questions as the apartment fell into silence. The tension remained, but amidst the uncertainty, he was determined to uncover the truth about the recent attacks and the enigmatic situation surrounding Pippa's sudden departure. Bruce paced back and forth in the apartment, his mind still grappling with the encounter with Pippa and the enigmatic situation surrounding her sudden departure. While their conversation had shed some light on the attacks they were investigating, he couldn't shake the feeling that he had only scratched the surface of the puzzle, especially regarding Pippa's involvement. There were still so many unanswered questions. What was Pippa hiding? Why did she seem to know more than she had let on? And what did her cryptic statement about his "slowly walking himself to hell" mean? As he mulled over the situation, Bruce realized he needed to approach the investigation from multiple angles. Gathering more evidence and clues would be crucial to understanding the bigger picture. He knew he couldn't rely solely on Pippa's words, as her recent actions had demonstrated that more might be beneath the surface. Bruce took a deep breath, focusing on the path ahead. He resolved to continue his investigation, leaving no stone unturned. He would retrace his steps, revisit crime scenes, talk to witnesses, and analyze any leads he had gathered so far. He'd also have to be more discreet about his findings to avoid further complicating his relationship with Pippa and to protect her if needed. The detective also knew he must carefully approach Detective Elaine Murphy of Montebello PD. While she might have valuable insights and information, Bruce had to be cautious about how much he revealed, especially given the high-stakes nature of the case. He pulled out his notebook and began jotting down new leads and questions from his recent conversation with Pippa. The more he thought about it, the more he realized that the truth they sought might not be as straightforward as they had initially thought.As Bruce continued to investigate, he couldn't help but feel a sense of urgency. The recent attacks were escalating, and lives were at stake. He knew he couldn't afford to let personal conflicts or uncertainties hinder the pursuit of justice.With determination in his heart, Bruce set out to uncover the missing pieces of the puzzle. He was determined to find the truth about the attacks and Pippa's involvement, regardless of the risks involved. Only then could he understand the full scope of the darkness they were facing and work towards bringing those responsible to justice. Bruce's resolve strengthened as he acknowledged the need for caution and thoroughness in his investigation. Jumping to conclusions without concrete evidence would only lead to confusion and potential misjudgment. He knew he couldn't rely solely on what he had seen in Pippa's apartment or the slip of her tongue during their heated exchange. To establish Pippa's true involvement in the attacks, Bruce understood that he needed a more comprehensive understanding of the situation. He would need to gather additional evidence, explore different leads, and consider alternative explanations. Patience, keen observation, and resourcefulness would be essential in unraveling the truth. Bruce made a mental note to review the information he had collected thus far, analyzing it from different angles and perspectives. He would cross-reference his findings, looking for patterns, connections, or discrepancies that could shed light on Pippa's role or any hidden agendas. In addition, Bruce knew he couldn't overlook other potential sources of information. He would revisit crime scenes, interview witnesses, and delve deeper into the victims' backgrounds. Every detail could be crucial in uncovering the truth and understanding the bigger picture. As Bruce continued his investigation, he remained vigilant, questioning his biases and being open to alternative possibilities. He recognized the importance of maintaining an objective and unbiased perspective, allowing the evidence to guide him rather than his emotions or assumptions. While uncertainty still lingered, Bruce's determination remained steadfast. He would gather the evidence, connect the dots, and only then draw conclusions based on the facts. No matter how elusive, the truth would eventually be revealed, and he would see justice served.

# CHAPTER SIX

**B**ruce carefully examined a crime scene at a building he was called to. The building was closed down due to an attack. He noticed several familiar signs that raised his suspicions. Despite the high crime rate in the County of Essex, he realizes that murder is not the most common crime in the area. Yet, the nature of the crime scene and the specific details he observed led him to believe that the same assailant might have targeted him alone in the past and, more recently, with Pippa. The similarities between the two incidents were striking to Bruce. The particular modus operandi, the way the crime scenes are set up, and specific distinct patterns all point to the involvement of a single perpetrator. The evidence suggested a deliberate intention to replicate the previous attack on Bruce, this time involving Pippa. Bruce realized that the assailant must have had a personal vendetta against him and orchestrated these attacks for some specific reason. He considered the possibility that Pippa might be an unwitting pawn in a larger scheme or that she could have some connection to the assailant. However, he has yet to determine the exact nature of their relationship. With the realization that he and Pippa have become targets of a calculated attacker, Bruce understood the gravity of the situation. He resolved to delve deeper into the investigation, determined to uncover the motives behind the attacks and ensure their safety.

As Bruce grappled with the realization that the initial murder attempt on him had now escalated to affect the entire County of Essex, a torrent of questions flooded his mind. He wondered who the next target would be and the perpetrator's ultimate motives. The scope and scale of the situation became increasingly shocking to him.

Bruce unexpectedly spotted Detective Elaine Murphy in a different part of the building amid these thoughts. He could not dismiss or reject her outright despite his anger and frustration. There was something about her that he still believed in or wanted to trust, even though he was questioning her involvement or information. Bruce approached

Detective Murphy, his expression reflecting anger and concern. With a tone of intensity in his voice, he addressed her, "Detective Murphy, we need to talk. I have serious questions about what's happening, and I need your help to find the answers." Though his initial instinct might have been to distance himself from her, Bruce recognized that he needed all the information and support he could get to navigate the escalating crisis. He hoped that engaging with Detective Murphy would shed light on the larger picture and allow them to work together to uncover the truth behind the attacks and the assailant's intentions. As Detective Christopher Hunter witnessed Bruce's confronting Detective Elaine Murphy, he shared Bruce's sentiments and frustration. In a burst of anger, Detective Christopher raised his voice and yelled directly at Detective Murphy, "Get out of my town! Detective Murphy, unfazed by the outburst, responded with a subtle smile. She didn't engage in an argument or attempt to defend herself. Instead, she calmly turned around and left Detectives Christopher and Bruce standing there, their emotions still running high. Before exiting, Detective Murphy left them with a cryptic remark, saying, "Every dog has its day!" Her words hung in the air, leaving an air of uncertainty and intrigue. It suggested there might be more to her actions and motivations than meets the eye. Detectives Christopher and Bruce exchanged glances, both bewildered by Detective Murphy's enigmatic response. They realized there was much more to uncover and understand about the situation, and they must remain vigilant in their pursuit of the truth. With a shared determination, they acknowledged that their paths may cross with Detective Murphy again, and they will need to navigate the complexities of their relationship to unravel the mysteries surrounding the escalating attacks in the County of Essex.

## CHAPTER SEVEN

**F**ollowing the discovery of Leonard Austin Frost's DNA at the scene of the murder, the urgency to apprehend him intensified. The incriminating evidence became compelling enough that a warrant was deemed unnecessary to proceed with his arrest and was fuelled by the speed to protect the public and bring the perpetrator to justice.

Law enforcement agencies remained resolute in swiftly apprehending Leonard; the escalating nature of the attacks and the potential threat he posed demanded immediate action.

Coordinated efforts were put into motion, with various law enforcement agencies pooling their resources and expertise to track Leonard down. Detectives, officers, and specialized units worked tirelessly, following leads, analyzing evidence, and conducting thorough investigations to locate and apprehend the suspect. The situation's urgency permeated the entire law enforcement community, and every effort was made to expedite the process. Police patrols were heightened, surveillance intensified, and informants were tapped into, aiming to determine Leonard's whereabouts and ensure his swift capture.

The community also played an active role, with law enforcement agencies relying on tips, information, and cooperation from concerned citizens. Public awareness campaigns were launched, urging citizens to remain vigilant and report any suspicious activity or sightings that could aid in locating Leonard.

With every passing moment, the pressure mounted on law enforcement to apprehend Leonard and end the reign of terror that had gripped Essex. The dedication and determination of law enforcement agencies were unwavering, as they worked day and night tirelessly to fulfill their duty to protect and serve.

As the search intensified, the streets of Essex became a battleground for justice. It was only a matter of time before Leonard Frost would be located, apprehended, and brought before the courts to face the consequences of his alleged crimes. The resolve of law enforcement remained unshaken, with the collective mission to restore peace and security to the city driving their every action.

Detectives Bruce and Christopher mobilized along with officers to locate and apprehend Leonard Austin Frost.

As they closed in on Leonard Austin Frost, the investigation became a race against time. Detectives Bruce and Christopher knew they needed to bring him in for questioning and gather further evidence to establish a watertight case against him. The discovery of his DNA at the crime scene was a significant step forward, but it was imperative to uncover the full extent of his involvement and motives.

Armed with the weight of the evidence against him, law enforcement agencies remained focused and relentless in their pursuit. The arrest of Leonard Austin Frost would provide answers and potentially prevent further harm to the community.

As the search intensified, the city of Capetown held its breath, anxiously awaiting the resolution of this gripping case that had consumed the town. The arrest of Leonard Austin Frost would mark a critical turning point in the investigation, bringing both closure and the promise of justice for the victims and their families.

Christopher was at his sparsely furnished apartment, poring over the information they'd gathered on Leonard Austin. The constant rain outside mirrored the murky atmosphere of their investigation, making the situation all the more oppressive.

His phone buzzed, breaking the silence. Christopher picked it up, glancing at the caller ID, which displayed a blocked number. He hesitated for a moment before answering, not knowing what to expect.

A gravelly voice on the other end spoke, "You've got your man. Austin is hiding in an abandoned safe house on Cargo Street. Move quickly, and you'll catch him."

Before he could speak, the phone call dropped.

Christopher's heart raced as he gave thought to the call. The voice on the other end unmistakably belonged to a confidential informant. He scribbled down the address on a notepad and thanked the informant before ending the call.

With newfound determination, he knew he needed to act swiftly. Christopher dialed Bruce's number, his voice crisp and urgent as he relayed the information, "Bruce, we've got a lead. Austin's hiding at the Cargo Street safe house. We need to move on this now."

Bruce, on the other end, didn't waste a moment. He acknowledged the information and hung up, reaching for his coat and pistol.

Within minutes, Christopher arrived at Bruce's apartment, where they met a special team Christopher had hastily assembled. The squad comprised seasoned Special Forces operatives, their faces concealed by tactical masks. The atmosphere was tense but focused.

"We've got the location. This is a high-risk mission," Bruce said as he briefed the team. "Christopher and I will lead you to the safe house. Our goal is to apprehend Austin without any casualties. Remember, we need him alive."

The squad members nodded in agreement, their determination evident in their eyes. As they prepared for the operation, the room buzzed with a sense of urgency.

Tactical gear was distributed, weapons were checked and loaded, and equipment was meticulously inspected. Flashlights, breaching tools, and first-aid kits were laid out in a precise formation. The room became a whirlwind of activity as the team readied themselves for the mission ahead.

As they geared up, Christopher, Sarge Ken, the squad leader, and Bruce went over the operation plan again, ensuring everyone knew their roles and the specifics of the mission. The rain outside intensified, drumming against the windows, a reminder of the impending danger they were about to face.

Once the team was fully equipped, they moved with precision and purpose. As they filed out of the apartment, each member in step, their gear making a symphony of clinks and rustles, it was a sight to behold. The convoy of black vehicles waited outside, engines idling, ready to whisk them away to the safe house. On their way, rain began its downpour.

The rain-slicked streets and the looming dark clouds seemed to be in perfect harmony with the gravity of their mission. Every second counted as they moved through the city, the road a winding trail of uncertainty that led to their target.

As they approached the safe house, the atmosphere grew heavier. The team members exchanged tense glances, fully aware of the danger that awaited them. They steeled themselves for what was to come, unwavering in their shared purpose and determination to apprehend Leonard Austin and unravel the truth.

The rain continued to pour, relentless and unforgiving, as if the heavens were witnessing the impending clash between law and darkness. The squad and the two determined detectives would soon confront the unknown, and the fate of their mission hung in the balance.

The abandoned safe house was a dilapidated structure, hidden amidst a tangle of overgrown trees and forgotten by time. Its windows were shattered, and the paint had peeled away long ago, leaving a skeletal frame that had seen better days. The wooden door hung askew on one rusty hinge, creaking ominously as it swayed in the breeze. Overhead, a slate-gray sky threatened rain, adding to the sense of foreboding that permeated the atmosphere.

The black SWAT vehicles pulled up quietly, tires whispering on the gravel road. The team, dressed in their tactical gear, emerged with purposeful precision. They moved silently, like phantoms in the dim light of dawn, to secure the area. Special Forces surrounded the safe house, ensuring that no civilians strayed too close. Their movements were coordinated and meticulous, clearing the vicinity with precision from countless training exercises.

Bruce and Christopher, waiting at a safe distance, gripped their firearms tightly. The tension in the air was palpable, a weight pressing down on them as they listened to the muffled commands and rustling of tactical gear.

Then, the moment arrived. Gunshots shattered the silence, followed by the screams of a desperate struggle from inside the safe house. Bruce and Christopher exchanged glances, their eyes reflecting the same concern and resolve.

Amidst the chaos, a figure emerged, dragging an almost unconscious Leonard Austin behind him. The SWAT leader, a formidable presence in the team, was a broad-shouldered man with a stern countenance, his eyes hidden behind reflective shades. He hauled Leonard with practiced efficiency, dragging him out into the open. Leonard's face was bruised, and his clothes were torn, bearing witness to the struggle inside.

Christopher leaned in toward Bruce, the tension etched on his face, and whispered, "That wasn't so hard, was it?" His words carried a mix of relief and disbelief, a sentiment shared between them as they watched the scene unfold.

Leonard was unceremoniously dumped into the back of one of the waiting SWAT trucks, his limp body slumping against the cold metal. The door slammed shut, echoing like a final, irrevocable judgment.

As the convoy departed, taking Leonard to the police station, the tension remained. The rain began to fall, a steady drizzle that matched the uncertainty of their next moves.

Inside the police station, Leonard was placed in a small, dimly lit room. He was given fresh clothes, but his gaze remained vacant, his spirit seemingly broken. The room was sparsely furnished, with a single table and two chairs, creating a stark atmosphere that mirrored the situation's intensity.

Meanwhile, outside the interrogation room, Bruce and Christopher spoke in hushed tones, deliberating who would interview the man behind the glass. They contemplated their next course of action, aware that Leonard's information could be their key to unraveling a much larger conspiracy.

The atmosphere in the police station was heavy with anticipation and apprehension. The clinking of handcuffs and the muted voices of officers created an eerie backdrop for the unfolding drama. The tension had only begun, and the stakes were higher than ever.

Detective Christopher Hunter took the lead in interrogating Leonard Austin Frost at the designated interrogation room in the County of Essex's PD. Determined to uncover the truth, he questioned Leonard Austin Frost extensively, hoping to reconcile the contradicting evidence and find answers.

During the interrogation, Leonard Austin Frost vehemently denied being anywhere near the crime scenes, presenting an alibi supported by his neighbors. According to them, they had seen Leonard Austin Frost with his children during the hours when the murders occurred. The accounts seemed credible, leaving Detectives Christopher Hunter and Bruce with doubts about Leonard's direct involvement.

The detectives couldn't ignore that Leonard's DNA, including hair strands and fingerprints, had been found at the crime scenes. This puzzling evidence remained unexplained, creating a significant discrepancy between Leonard's alibis and the forensic findings.

Amidst the conflicting information, Adams Gibson, the Chief of County of Essex PD, held a distinct perspective. He firmly believed that Leonard Austin Frost was concealing something, suggesting that the lumberman strategically used his alibis to mask his genuine involvement in the crimes.

Detectives Bruce and Christopher Hunter were torn between the seemingly convincing alibis and the concrete DNA evidence. They recognized the need for further investigation and sought to uncover any hidden connections or motives that could explain the presence of Leonard's DNA at the crime scenes.

As the investigation continued, the detectives knew they had to dig deeper, explore alternative angles, and gather additional evidence to corroborate or challenge Leonard's alibis. The case was far from closed, and the truth behind the conflicting evidence and Leonard's potential involvement remained elusive, awaiting their relentless pursuit of justice.

Bruce, determined to get to the bottom of the perplexing situation, directed a straightforward question at Leonard: "Do you know anyone who might want to implicate you by planting your DNA at these crime scenes?"

Leonard, taken aback by the question, registered shock and realization. His response carried an unexpected shock factor of its own. With a tense pause, he finally spoke, his voice filled with a hint of revelation, "I think I do!"

The room fell silent as Bruce and Detective Christopher Hunter exchanged surprised glances. This unexpected declaration opened up a new avenue of investigation, potentially revealing a motive and shedding light on the mysterious circumstances surrounding Leonard's DNA being found at the crime scenes.

Recognizing the significance of Leonard's statement, Bruce leaned in, his voice earnest and probing, "Who do you think might want to implicate you, and why?"

Leonard hesitated, contemplating his response carefully before finally speaking.

"There's a longstanding feud between my family and the Martellis. We've had differences, and I suspect they might be behind this. They've always held a grudge against us."

Bruce and Detective Christopher Hunter exchanged another glance; a shared understanding formed between them. The possibility of a vendetta between the two families added a layer of complexity to the investigation. It introduced a motive that could explain the intentional planting of Leonard's DNA at the crime scenes.

Realizing that this new lead needed to be thoroughly explored, Bruce and Detective Christopher Hunter made a mental note to delve into the history between the Frost and Martelli families. Uncovering the truth behind this feud could bring them closer to solving the mystery and identifying the culprit behind the attacks in the County of Essex.

With renewed determination, the detectives continued their relentless pursuit of justice, driven by the revelation that there may be more to the story than meets the eye. The tangled web of motives, alliances, and betrayals was beginning to unravel, inching them closer to the truth they had been tirelessly seeking.

# CHAPTER EIGHT

A s Leonard revealed his concerns about potential individuals who could implicate him, his plea for protection from law enforcement agencies echoed with urgency. Understanding the gravity of his situation, Leonard recognized the need to safeguard himself from any possible harm or retaliation from these individuals.

Seeking assurance and a sense of security, Leonard turned to law enforcement agencies, hoping they would provide the necessary protection. He understood that his cooperation in the investigation was crucial, but he also knew his safety was paramount. Leonard needed to ensure he could provide the information without fear of reprisals that could jeopardize his well-being.

With a sense of trepidation and vulnerability, Leonard reached out to the authorities, seeking their assistance and the reassurance that they would take the necessary steps to protect him.

His gaze flickered from the table to Christopher's face. He broke the silence, his voice strained with desperation and fear. "You've got to promise me something, Agent Christopher."

Christopher leaned forward, his expression serious. "What is it, Leonard? Speak."

Leonard hesitated before he spoke, choosing his words carefully. "You have to protect me and my family. If the man behind this realizes I've been taken in, he'll stop at nothing to eliminate us, to erase any trace."

Christopher understood the gravity of Leonard's request. The dangerous criminal they were pursuing had shown no mercy in the past. Leonard's life and the lives of his family were hanging by a thread.

After a brief pause, Christopher nodded and replied, "Okay, macho, I promise you, if you continue to cooperate, we will do everything in our power to ensure your safety and your family's safety. They will be heavily guarded indefinitely until this whole operation is done."

Relief washed over Leonard's face as he exhaled a long-held breath. He knew there was a glimmer of hope even in the shadow of danger. His cooperation was their lifeline, and Christopher's promise was their lifeline's lifeline.

Understanding the severity of the situation, law enforcement agencies assessed Leonard's request seriously. They evaluated the credibility of his claims, gathered additional information to corroborate his story, and determined if protection, such as relocation, surveillance, or the assignment of a personal security detail, was necessary.

To ensure Leonard's safety, the law enforcement agencies worked closely with him, keeping him informed about the progress of their investigation and any developments related to his protection. They strove to create an environment where Leonard could provide crucial information without compromising his well-being.

Leonard's plea for protection did not go unheard. The authorities recognized the significance of his cooperation and took the necessary measures to safeguard him from potential harm. Through collaboration and careful execution of security protocols, they provided Leonard with the reassurance and protection he desperately sought.

The County of Essex PD, responsible for Leonard's case, approached his plea for protection with caution and responsibility. They understood the need to validate his provided leads before committing to protective measures. The authorities recognized that the credibility and significance of Leonard's information would be crucial in determining the level of protection he would receive.

The Essex PD initiated a thorough investigation into the leads Leonard provided. They carefully evaluated the integrity of the information, cross-referencing it with their existing knowledge and conducting further inquiries to corroborate the details. The authorities understood the importance of relying on concrete evidence and genuine threats to ensure the appropriate allocation of resources and protection.

During this investigation, the Essex PD employed various techniques, such as gathering additional intelligence, interviewing relevant individuals, and analyzing potential connections or patterns. They also worked closely with other law enforcement agencies, sharing information and collaborating to understand the situation comprehensively.

As the investigation progressed, the authorities kept Leonard informed about their progress. They maintained open lines of communication, updating him on the validation process and any developments related to his case. Transparency was the key to building trust and assuring Leonard that his safety was being taken seriously.

By prioritizing the validation of leads and the credibility of threats, the Essex PD aimed to provide Leonard with the appropriate protection while maintaining the integrity of their investigation. Their thorough approach helped ensure that any actions taken were based on protecting Leonard from potential harm.n sound judgment, maximizing the chances of uncovering the truth while safeguarding

In response to Leonard's plea, the County of Essex PD assured him that if his leads were deemed valid and supported by substantial evidence, they would take the necessary steps to provide him with the protection he sought. The safety and security of witnesses and informants are of utmost importance to law enforcement agencies, as they play a crucial role in pursuing justice.

However, the authorities clarified that Leonard's claims would be thoroughly investigated before any protective measures were implemented. This approach was necessary to ensure that false leads or attempts to manipulate the situation would not compromise the integrity of the investigation or the safety of innocent individuals.

The County of Essex PD pledged its commitment to uncovering the truth and ensuring the safety of all parties involved while maintaining the principles of due process and impartiality. They would meticulously evaluate Leonard's information, relying on diligent investigation and corroborating evidence to determine the veracity of his claims before proceeding with any protective measures.

By adhering to these protocols, law enforcement agencies aimed to balance the need for Leonard's safety with the imperative of uncovering the whole truth behind the escalating attacks. Their approach would help minimize potential risks and ensure justice was served relatively and comprehensively.

As Leonard shared the first name on his list of individuals who might be interested in implicating him, Leonard George, a clearer picture began to emerge. Leonard George, the Head of Forestry at Dream Farms, held a position of authority within the company that oversees the tree farm owned by Leonard Austin Frost.

Leonard suggested that his refusal to participate in a wood supply fraud within the Supply Unit could have made Leonard George seek his removal, implicating him in the crimes and explaining why his DNA may have been planted there. This revelation unveiled a potential motive for crime scenes.

Law enforcement agencies, including the County of Essex PD, recognized the significance of this lead and the need to investigate Leonard George's possible involvement thoroughly. If Leonard's claims could be substantiated, it could uncover a web of corruption and illicit activities within Dream Farms.

The authorities diligently pursued this lead, gathering evidence and conducting interviews to determine the veracity of Leonard's allegations. They worked to establish a clear connection between Leonard George and the crimes, ensuring that justice would be served and the truth would be brought to light.

Simultaneously, the County of Essex PD took the necessary precautions to protect Leonard, keeping him safe from potential harm or retaliation. His information could be crucial in solving the case and dismantling any criminal activities within Dream Farms.

As the investigation proceeded, the authorities gathered information, weighed the evidence, and determined the appropriate action. They remained committed to upholding the law, ensuring the safety of all involved parties, and uncovering the truth behind the escalating attacks in Essex. As Leonard revealed the second person on his list, Jeff Griffin, a new layer of complexity was added to the investigation. Jeff Griffin, an investment banker who only visited the County of Essex on weekends, had been embroiled in a longstanding conflict with Leonard Austin Frost. Jeff strongly believed that Leonard was responsible for the death of his sister, who was also his wife.

This longstanding feud between Jeff and Leonard presented another potential motive for someone to implicate Leonard in the crimes. Leonard suspected that Jeff might have orchestrated the planting of his DNA at the crime scenes to divert attention away from Leonard and involve him instead.

Though not entirely hopeful about these leads, Detective Bruce understood the significance of exploring every possible avenue in the investigation. He recognized that even seemingly unlikely authorities could sometimes lead to unexpected breakthroughs. Therefore, he remained committed to thoroughly investigating Leonard

George and Jeff Griffin, seeking to uncover any evidence linking them to the crimes.

With cautious optimism, Detective Bruce delved into the backgrounds of both individuals, examining their motives, previous conflicts, and potential access to the crime scenes. He gathered evidence, interviewed witnesses, and worked alongside his colleagues to determine the validity of Leonard's claims.

While cautious, Detective Bruce understood the importance of thoroughly exploring these leads. It is through meticulous investigation and the pursuit of every possible connection that the truth can be uncovered, justice served, and the safety of innocent individuals ensured.

The investigation continued, fuelled by the determination to uncover the truth behind the escalating attacks in Essex. As Detective Bruce and his team delved deeper into the lives of Leonard George and Jeff Griffin, they remained vigilant, knowing that answers might lie within the intricate web of personal conflicts and agendas.

## CHAPTER NINE

**B**ruce sat in the bustling café, his hands wrapped around the steaming cup of coffee, trying to escape the scorching heat outside. As he watched the world go by, he was drawn suddenly to a familiar figure in the distance. Detective Elaine Murphy was a renowned investigator known for her brilliant deductive skills.

Curiosity piqued, Bruce set his coffee down and discreetly observed Detective Murphy as she made her way through the crowded café. She seemed focused, her eyes scanning the surroundings with purpose. Bruce's interest grew, wondering where she might be heading and what had caught her attention in this seemingly ordinary café.

Bruce couldn't help but feel the excitement as Detective Murphy neared his table. He had always been fascinated by mysteries and detective work, and here was an opportunity to witness a skilled investigator in action. Detective Murphy briefly glanced in Bruce's direction, her eyes sharp and observant. Bruce quickly averted his gaze, not wanting to appear intrusive. But the detective's presence intrigued him, and he couldn't resist the urge to find out more.

Carefully, Bruce followed Detective Murphy from a distance, keeping her within sight. She determinedly maneuvered through the bustling streets, her pace steady and purposeful. Bruce's curiosity intensified, wondering where her destination might be.

After a few blocks, Detective Murphy entered a dilapidated building tucked away in a quiet alley. Bruce hesitated, contemplating whether to continue following her or to let the mystery be. However, his adventurous spirit got the better, and he decided to take a chance.

Bruce cautiously approached the building, his steps light and careful. Peering through a cracked window, he could see Detective Murphy conversing with a group of individuals. They appeared to be discussing something of great importance, their expressions severe and focused.

Intrigued and determined to uncover the truth, Bruce found an open door and entered the building. He moved stealthily, careful not to disturb the ongoing conversation. As he approached the group, his heart raced with anticipation.

Maintaining his composure, Bruce met Detective Murphy's gaze with a calm expression. He understood her surprise and the need for her to ascertain his intentions.

"Hello, it's nice to see you again." he held his right arm up, a show of getting, his tone respectful and sincere. "I'm here because I've been closely following the recent string of attacks. I am interested in seeking justice, and I believe there might be connections between these cases and other information I've encountered."

Bruce paused for a moment, choosing his words carefully before continuing. "I've been investigating, gathering evidence, and exploring leads. I'm committed to uncovering the truth and assisting in any way possible."

He met Detective Murphy's eyes, hoping to convey his genuine curiosity and desire to contribute to the investigation. Bruce understood the importance of establishing trust and credibility with the detective, especially considering his concrete involvement in the case.

"I understand that this may seem unusual, but I assure you that my intentions are solely focused on finding answers and helping bring those responsible to justice," Bruce added, hoping to alleviate Detective Murphy's concerns.

Bruce awaited Detective Murphy's response, ready to provide additional information or clarify any questions she might have.

Detective Murphy studied Bruce for a moment, her gaze penetrating yet thoughtful. After a brief pause, she nodded. "Normally, I wouldn't involve other detectives in my case, but your enthusiasm is hard to ignore," she said. "If you truly are passionate about this work, perhaps you can assist. But be warned, this investigation is not for the faint of heart."

A rush of excitement surged through Bruce as he realized the incredible opportunity ahead. He nodded eagerly, ready to embark on an unexpected journey alongside Detective Elaine Murphy, knowing he was about to delve into a world of intrigue, danger, and the unknown.

And so, Bruce's life took an unforeseen turn as he joined forces with the seasoned detective. Little did he know that their partnership would test his mettle, push the boundaries of his courage, and challenge his abilities as they unraveled a complex case that would leave an indelible mark on both of their lives.

Bruce followed Detective Murphy as she made her way to an apartment complex on Silicon Boulevard. His curiosity was piqued as he wondered what awaited him in this mysterious location. Keeping a safe distance, he observed her enter the building and head toward the garage.

Bruce discreetly made his way to a vantage point where he could observe the garage without being noticed. From his concealed position, he watched Detective Murphy meet a man inside. Their conversation seemed intense, their body language suggesting secrecy and urgency.

Realizing the significance of the situation, Bruce reached for his phone and discreetly snapped a photo of the exchange. He wanted to capture evidence of this suspicious meeting in case it would be helpful later.

Once Detective Murphy left the garage, Bruce bided his time, waiting for the opportune moment to investigate further. He wanted to uncover the truth behind this mysterious encounter. With caution and determination, he approached the garage and carefully inspected the surroundings.

As Bruce entered the garage, he discovered signs that the man and Detective Murphy had been discussing something important. Papers scattered across a workbench, a laptop left unattended, and a map pinned to a wall caught his attention. It seemed like they were involved in a detailed investigation.

Bruce couldn't resist the temptation to dig deeper, driven by his thirst for knowledge and his desire to assist in unraveling the truth. He began examining the documents and searching through the digital files on the laptop, hoping to find any clues that would shed light on the situation.

As he delved further into the man's belongings, Bruce discovered encrypted files and coded messages, indicating the complexity of the investigation at hand. He knew he had stumbled upon something significant, but the full extent of it still eluded him.

Aware that time was of the essence, Bruce carefully documented his findings, taking notes and photographs to share with Detective Murphy later. He understood the importance of maintaining the investigation's integrity and relaying all relevant information correctly to the authorities.

With the evidence securely gathered, Bruce decided to leave the garage and regroup at home. He knew that sharing his discoveries with Detective Murphy would be crucial in helping her connect the dots and solve the mystery at hand.

Leaving the apartment, Bruce's mind raced with possibilities. He couldn't help but wonder about the implications of his findings and how they would impact the ongoing investigation. Little did he know that his involvement would soon thrust him into a world of danger and intrigue, where his determination to uncover the truth would be tested.

Bruce had left the garage but not with a brown wallet he had seen half open while he rummaged through the table, clutched in his hand. He couldn't wait to get home and examine its contents thoroughly, but his empty stomach had other plans. He decided to stop at a small, fast restaurant on his way.

Seated at a corner booth, he placed the wallet on the table and ordered a meal. The aroma of sizzling food filled the air as he watched the rain trickle down the window, lost in thought.

Bruce's gaze drifted back to the wallet as he bit into his meal. He couldn't help but wonder about the man whose ID he had found. How was he connected to Elaine? Why had she been so intent on uncovering the truth about him?

The wallet lay open, revealing the ID with an ordinary and enigmatic face. Bruce pondered the possibilities, his mind racing through various scenarios.

After a few minutes, he carefully slipped the ID back into the wallet, returning it to his pocket. There would be time to delve deeper into the man's identity later. He needed sustenance and a moment of respite to gather his thoughts.

With his meal finished, Bruce signaled for the check, paid, and then headed out into the night, the rain-slicked streets glistening under the glow of the city's lights. He hailed a cab, the ID securely in his possession, and made his way home.

Bruce left the restaurant with urgency, the wallet safely tucked into his jacket pocket. He had just discovered a vital piece of the puzzle, which fuelled his determination to unravel the connections between the mysterious man and Elaine.

The rain had subsided, leaving the city streets glistening under the streetlights. Bruce hailed a cab, slipping into the backseat, his mind occupied with thoughts of the man whose ID he now possessed. As the taxi navigated through the winding streets, he couldn't help but wonder how deep this rabbit hole went. The ID was a mere breadcrumb; he knew he was far from uncovering the whole story.

Upon arriving home, Bruce stepped into his cozy, dimly lit apartment. It was a welcome retreat from the chaos of his investigation. He kicked off his shoes and settled into a well-worn armchair, allowing the silence to wash over him. He contemplated the ID in his pocket, the face on the photograph staring back at him with a sense of secrecy.

But he needed a good night's rest to face the next day's challenges. Bruce decided to put off further examination of the ID until morning, as his weary mind needed rest to process the new information.

The following day, Bruce awoke with a renewed sense of purpose. He went through his morning routine, the warm water from the shower revitalizing him. Dressed in a crisp suit and a well-ironed shirt, he retrieved the ID from his jacket pocket. He double-checked the address, ensuring it was memorized to the street number. He knew he had to arrive early to catch the man at home.

Before leaving his apartment, he prepared a quick breakfast—a scrambled egg and toast, his concentration never wavering from the task. The ID lay on the kitchen counter, a constant reminder of the mission he was about to undertake.

With breakfast consumed, he left his apartment and hailed a taxi, providing the driver with the address he'd carefully memorized. The city was still half-asleep, the streets quiet, and the day's first light breaking through the clouds.

The taxi moved through the city, bringing him closer to the destination. Bruce's mind was a whirlwind of thoughts and anticipation. He couldn't help but wonder what awaited him at the address, what secrets it might hold, and how it connected to Elaine.

The cab pulled up to a nondescript building, and Bruce paid the fare before stepping out onto the sidewalk. He took a deep breath, gathering his resolve. With the ID clutched firmly in his hand, he approached the entrance. It was a pivotal moment, a step further down the path that might ultimately lead to the answers he sought.

Bruce's determination to uncover the truth led him to barge into the man's place, hoping to extract any hidden information from him. With adrenaline coursing through his veins, he prepared to confront him head-on.

As Bruce entered the room, tension filled the air. The man instinctively moved to defend himself, startled by the intrusion, asking who he was and why he barged into his house. Bruce's frustration boiled over, and he resorted to physical force in his quest for answers. As Bruce pressed the man to reveal if he knew who Detective Murphy was and why they had been seeing, punches and jabs were exchanged.

Amidst the struggle, the man remained steadfast in his claim. He insisted that he was an architect and that his involvement with Detective Murphy revolved solely around acquiring the plans for a specific building. Despite the physical confrontation, his story did not waver.

As the situation's intensity subsided, Bruce's rational side began to emerge. He took a step back, assessing the situation more objectively. Doubts started to creep into his mind. Was he being too aggressive in his pursuit of the truth? Could there be another explanation for Detective Murphy's coming to see him?

Taking a deep breath, Bruce decided to shift his approach. Instead of resorting to violence, he chose dialogue to extract information. He sat down with the man, physically and emotionally exhausted, and sought a calmer conversation.

Bruce probed further to understand the connection between the architect and Detective Murphy. He asked detailed questions, trying to unravel the underlying truth behind their collaboration. Still, on edge, the man began to open up about their shared involvement in obtaining the plans for a specific building.

According to the man's account, Detective Murphy had sought his architectural expertise to help gather information about a building associated with a complex case she was investigating. He claimed that his role was purely professional, aimed at aiding her in understanding the structure's layout and potential hidden areas.

Bruce's skepticism began to wane as the man's explanations aligned with the evidence he had discovered earlier. The encrypted files, coded messages, and the intense discussion he had witnessed between Detective Murphy and the man in the garage all seemed to point toward a real investigative purpose.

Bruce shifted his perspective, realizing his initial assumptions might have been misguided. He acknowledged that Detective Murphy had her reasons for keeping the details of her investigation confidential, even from someone like him who had shown genuine interest.

Relieved by the weight of suspicion, Bruce decided to leave the man's place. He thanked him for sharing his side of the story and apologized for the aggression he had displayed earlier. As he walked away, he contemplated how easily assumptions and a desire for the truth could blur the line between justice and injustice.

Bruce now understood that a commitment to her investigation drove Detective Murphy's actions, and he had unintentionally crossed a line in his quest for answers. This experience would serve as a valuable lesson, reminding him of the importance of balance, respect, and trust in pursuing truth and justice. The architect's account of helping Detective Murphy obtain plans for a specific building intrigued Bruce, who decided to inquire further. With a cautious tone, he brought up the address of the building, subtly hinting at his knowledge without revealing the source of his information. "So, the building you helped Detective Murphy with is located at [address]?"

Bruce asked, carefully observing the architect's reaction.

The architect's face tightened slightly, and an unease flickered across his features. He hesitated momentarily before responding, "Yes, that's the one. How did you know that address?"

Bruce remained mysterious about the source of his information, not wanting to disclose his involvement with the County of Essex's architectural black market. Instead, he chose to focus on the bigger picture.

"Well, I've been doing some research of my own, trying to understand the bigger picture," Bruce explained, his voice tinged with curiosity. "It seems that Detective Murphy has been quite secretive about this investigation. Do you have any insights into what she might be up to?"

The architect sighed, appearing conflicted. He glanced around the room as if assessing the level of trust he could place in Bruce. After a moment, he decided to share a fragment of the truth.

"I can't say for certain what Detective Murphy's exact intentions are, but I can tell you that the building in question holds a hidden secret," the architect confessed, his voice laced with caution.

"There are rumors of illegal activities taking place within its walls. Some say it's a hub for organized crime or a base for a secretive group."

Bruce's interest heightened as he absorbed the architect's words. The notion that Detective Murphy might investigate a hidden underbelly within the building intrigued him further. He wondered how deep the rabbit hole went and what other secrets the architect might know.

Realizing that the architect might possess more valuable information, Bruce pressed further, his voice laced with curiosity and a hint of urgency.

"Are there any specific details or leads you can provide about the activities in that building?" Bruce probed, hoping to uncover more of the puzzle.

The architect hesitated, contemplating the risks of divulging further information. Eventually, he nodded, understanding Bruce's curiosity and thirst for the truth.

"Look, I can't give you much more without putting myself in jeopardy," the architect warned, his eyes filled with caution. "But I can say that Detective Murphy has been digging deep, trying to expose the dark underbelly within that building. Her pursuit of justice is relentless, and she's treading on dangerous ground."

Bruce absorbed the architect's words, realizing his suspicions about Detective Murphy were unfounded. He now understood that her covert actions were driven by a desire to uncover the truth and bring those responsible to justice.

Armed with this newfound knowledge, Bruce contemplated his next move. He knew that his involvement in the investigation had crossed ethical boundaries, but his desire to assist Detective Murphy in her pursuit of justice burned more vital than ever.

Little did he know that his determination to uncover the hidden truth would draw him further into a web of danger, secrets, and unexpected revelations. The path ahead was uncertain, but Bruce was prepared to face the consequences and help shed light on the mysteries that shrouded the enigmatic building and Detective Elaine Murphy's true intentions.

# CHAPTER TEN

Pippa and Bruce stood in the middle of Pippa's living room, their faces flushed with anger and frustration. The sun's rays illuminated the room, but their heated exchange cast a shadow over the tranquility of the morning.

With her fiery red hair, Pippa clenched her fists tightly, her voice filled with determination. "Bruce, I can't take this anymore! Every day, it's the same argument, the same fights. We can't keep living like this!"

Bruce, his brows furrowed, responded with equal intensity. "Oh, and it's all my fault. You never take responsibility for your actions. It's always me who has to apologize and make things right!"

Their words clashed, each accusation fuelling the fire between them. Pippa paced back and forth, her voice shaking with pent-up emotions. "You never listen to me, Bruce! You always dismiss my feelings and opinions. It's like I don't even matter to you!"

Bruce's frustration grew, his voice rising. "And what about you, Pippa? You're so stubborn, never willing to compromise. You must always be right, even when you're wrong!"

Their voices reverberated through the room, the air heavy with tension. They had been through countless arguments, each time vowing to work things out but somehow ending up in the same destructive cycle.

Pippa's eyes welled up with tears, her voice quivering. "I don't want us to end up hating each other, Bruce. We need to find a way to communicate better, to understand each other."

Bruce's anger softened momentarily as he looked into Pippa's teary eyes. "I don't want to lose you either, Pippa. But we can't keep repeating the same patterns. We need to change."

Silence fell upon them, the weight of their words hanging in the air. They realized that something needed to give, that their relationship could not survive on constant arguments and unresolved issues. The morning sun, once a symbol of hope, now highlighted the cracks in their bond.

In that moment of realization, they made a silent commitment to seek help, work on their communication, and learn to understand one another honestly. They knew it wouldn't be easy, but their love and the desire to make it work outweighed the pain of their ongoing conflicts.

As they took a deep breath, their eyes met, and a glimmer of hope sparked between them. They knew their journey toward healing and growth would be challenging, but they were determined to embark on it together.

Suddenly, Bruce's phone rang. "Hello, is this Bruce?" a voice on the other end of the line asked, a hint of urgency evident in their tone.

Bruce's heart skipped a beat. The unexpected call only heightened his already mounting apprehension. "Yes, this is Bruce. Who is this?"

"It's Officer Johnson from the local police department. I'm sorry to disturb you, but we have some important information regarding your sister, Emily," the voice explained, causing Bruce's anxiety to spike.

Bruce's mind raced with worry. Emily had been going through a difficult time lately, and he had been trying to support her as best he could. The sudden call from the police only added to his concerns.

"What happened? Is Emily okay?" Bruce's voice trembled, his concern evident.

Officer Johnson took a moment before responding, his voice measured. "We found Emily in her apartment this morning. She was unresponsive, and the paramedics were called.

They're currently at the scene, trying to stabilize her. We thought it best to inform you as her next of kin."

Shock washed over Bruce as he struggled to process the news. Sensing something was wrong, Pippa approached him with worry across her face. He held up a hand to signal her to wait, then returned to the phone.

"I...I appreciate your letting me know, Officer Johnson. Is she going to be all right? Can I go see her?" Bruce's voice cracked with concern.

"I'm afraid I don't have all the details yet, but I suggest you come to the hospital as soon as possible. They will be able to provide you with more information there," Officer Johnson replied with sympathy.

Bruce hung up the phone, his mind swirling with emotions. He turned to Pippa, tears welling up in his eyes. "It's Emily. Something's happened to her. We need to go to the hospital right away."

Pippa's features softened, her worries set aside as she embraced Bruce. "I'm so sorry, Bruce. Let's go. We'll be there for her."

Their previous argument now seemed insignificant as they hurriedly gathered their belongings and rushed out the door, focusing entirely on supporting Emily in her time of need. The morning sun, once a symbol of a new day, now carried a weight of uncertainty as they embarked on a different journey that would test their strength, resilience, and relationship bonds.

Bruce's hand tightened around the receiver as he recounted each word the solemn voice had delivered– Another murder, this time at the train station. Panic surged through his veins; his eyes widened with terror. Sensing the gravity of the conversation, Pippa approached him cautiously, her anger dissipating in the face of Bruce's distress.

Bruce's mind raced as the voice on the other end of the line provided further details. He struggled to comprehend the unfolding tragedy and its potential implications. The train station, which he had passed countless times, had become a haunting backdrop for a heinous crime.

Pippa reached out, placing a comforting hand on Bruce's trembling shoulder. Her eyes mirrored his concern and fear, intertwining their emotions in a shared sense of vulnerability. "Bruce, what's happened? Are you okay?" she asked, her voice filled with genuine concern.

Bruce's voice quivered as he relayed the distressing news to Pippa. "There has been another murder at the train station. It's... it's a terrifying thought, Pippa. I can't believe this is happening."

Pippa's grip on his shoulder tightened, offering silent support. "We need to stay calm, Bruce. Let's gather more information and find out what's going on. Maybe there's something we can do to help or stay safe."

Bruce nodded, his mind filled with a mix of fear and determination. He knew they couldn't allow themselves to be consumed by panic and needed to gather their wits and respond thoughtfully to the situation.

They quickly switched on the television, hoping to find news coverage providing more information about the incident. The screen displayed chaotic scenes of police vehicles, yellow tape, and concerned onlookers. Reporters were trying to piece together the limited details available, their voices echoing the shock and uncertainty that gripped the city.

Bruce's heart raced as he absorbed the gravity of the situation. The safety and well-being of the community, as well as their own, hung in the balance. He knew they couldn't stand idly by, waiting for more information. They had to take action.

"Pippa, we can't just sit here. We need to ensure our safety and see if there's anything we can do to help," Bruce said, his voice laced with determination.

Pippa nodded, her eyes reflecting both concern and resolve. "You're right, Bruce. We'll stay vigilant and take necessary precautions. Let's contact friends, family, and authorities to gather more information and offer assistance."

Hand in hand, they ventured into the uncertain day ahead, their bond strengthened by shared fear and a mutual commitment to protect each other and their community. As the morning sun continued its ascent, casting a fragile light on the unfolding events, Pippa and Bruce set out to navigate the darkness that had suddenly enveloped their city, hoping to find solace amidst the chaos and a way to restore peace.

The cab ride to the train station was a tense and silent one. Pippa and Bruce sat side by side, their minds occupied by the unfolding events. The cityscape passed in a blur, the streets lined with people going about their daily lives, unaware of the dark cloud over the train station.

Pippa couldn't help but fidget with her hands, her gaze drifting to the window. The rhythmic rain tapping against the car's roof added to the somber atmosphere. She glanced at Bruce, concern etched on her face. "Are you sure we're doing the right thing, Bruce? This feels dangerous, and we don't know what we're against."

Bruce sighed, his eyes fixed on the road ahead. "I understand your concerns, Pippa, but we can't ignore this. Lives are at stake, and we can make a difference. We need to be cautious and rely on our instincts."

Pippa nodded, her unease only partially eased. She had always admired his determination and commitment to justice, but this case felt different, more personal. She knew their journey into the heart of the investigation was fraught with risks, but she was willing to stand by his side.

The cab cut through the city's streets, eventually approaching the train station. As they drew nearer to the crime scene, the atmosphere inside the car grew heavier. It was a moment of quiet resolve as they prepared to confront the unknown.

Upon their arrival at the train station, they stepped out of the cab, the weight of their mission heavy on their shoulders. The station's platform was eerily deserted.

Pippa and Bruce stood at the train station entrance, their minds pounding with a mixture of apprehension and curiosity. The train station was typically a bustling hub of activity, but now it lay in eerie silence, surrounded by yellow police tape.

The scene was a chaotic blend of flashing police lights, bustling officers, and concerned onlookers. As they approached the crime scene, Bruce's eyes darted around, scanning for any clues or information that could shed light on the murder.

Pippa kept a close watch on him, her anxiety palpable. She trusted Bruce's instincts and experience, but the gravity of the situation weighed on her.

As they reached the station's center, they saw a small group of detectives huddled together. Bruce led the way, his demeanor severe and focused. The detectives acknowledged his presence with a nod, recognizing him as a former officer with a knack for solving cases.

Pippa observed from a distance, her eyes sweeping the area. The crime scene was cordoned off, and the victim's body had been taken away, but the faint trace of blood remained, stark against the station's pristine floors.

Bruce, engaged in conversation with the detectives, received their initial assessment. It was clear that this murder bore similarities to the previous one. The assailant's pattern was emerging, and fear hung heavily. There was a growing sense that the city was in the grip of a serial killer.

As the conversation with the detectives continued, Bruce's phone buzzed in his pocket. He excused himself and stepped aside to take the call, finding a quiet corner where he could speak without interruption.

Pippa watched him intently as he answered the call. Bruce's face grew grave, and he nodded in response to the voice on the other end of the line. The hushed conversation carried a sense of urgency, and Pippa couldn't help but wonder about the call's content.

Bruce's expression remained somber as he listened, a furrow of concern etched across his brow. He occasionally glanced in Pippa's direction, his eyes conveying the gravity of the situation.

Pippa felt a mixture of curiosity and unease. She couldn't hear the words of the conversation, but the tension in Bruce's stance was enough to convey the severity of the information he was receiving.

The call concluded, and Bruce returned to Pippa's side. He looked at her, his gaze filled with a sense of purpose. "We need to get back to the apartment, Pippa. There's been significant development, and we have to act quickly. I don't want to tell you here, and we need to be somewhere private."

Pippa nodded, sensing the urgency in his voice. She knew their involvement in this investigation was far from over and that the latest information had pushed them deeper into the mystery.

They left the train station, their footsteps echoing through the silent halls. The sun outside had given way to overcast skies, casting a somber hue over the city. As they stepped into a waiting cab, Pippa's mind raced with questions, but she understood that now was not the time for it.

Bruce looked into Pippa's eyes, the weight of the news heavy on his shoulders. He knew he had to share the unsettling message, as tricky as it was. Taking a deep breath to steady himself, he spoke with a voice filled with trepidation.

"Pippa, I need to tell you something, and it's not easy. I just received a call... It's about our dear friend, Sarah. She... she didn't make it."

Pippa's eyes widened in shock, her hand instinctively reaching out to Bruce for support. "What? No, that can't be true. Sarah... was such a vibrant soul. What happened?"

Bruce's voice cracked as he tried to convey the heart-breaking details. "There was a car accident last night. Sarah was involved, and... She didn't survive. I'm so sorry, Pippa. I can't believe it myself."

Tears welled up in Pippa's eyes, her body trembling with grief. The news struck her like a thunderbolt, shattering the tranquillity they had hoped for at the start of the day. Sarah, their dear friend, was gone, leaving an impossible void.

Bruce held Pippa close, offering solace in that moment of shared sorrow. They stood together, their embrace a fragile anchor amidst the storm of emotions.

During their grief, Pippa and Bruce found strength in each other. They knew they had to lean on their bond to navigate the painful journey ahead, supporting one another as they mourned the loss of their beloved friend.

They would remember Sarah's infectious laughter, kindness, and shared moments. They would honor her memory by cherishing their time with her and finding solace in the love and support they found in each other.

They found themselves at Pippa's apartment, seeking solace after the heart-breaking news about their friend Sarah. The air inside was thick with the lingering emotions of grief and disbelief. Pippa was seated in a chair, her face a mosaic of sadness and confusion, her thoughts racing through memories of their dear friend.

As Bruce moved about the apartment, he prepared a cup of coffee for Pippa. The familiar coffee-making routine was a comforting distraction from the harsh reality they had just learned. The scent of brewing coffee wafted through the room, filling the space with warmth.

With a cup in hand, Bruce sat down opposite Pippa. He looked into her eyes, his expression mixed with sympathy and concern. His voice was steady but heavy with the weight of the news he was about to deliver.

"Pippa," Bruce began, his tone soft yet committed, "there's something more I need to tell you. It isn't easy, but we need to be aware of it. The accident involving Sarah... it wasn't just an accident. Our loved ones, our friends, are now being targeted."

Pippa's eyes widened in alarm, her hands gripping the sides of her coffee cup. "Targeted? What do you mean, Bruce?"

Bruce took a deep breath before continuing. "I've been receiving information that there's a pattern emerging. Sarah's accident, along with recent incidents at the train station, seems to be connected. It's as if someone is deliberately causing harm, and we can't ignore the possibility that we might be next."

Pippa's heart raced, the implications of Bruce's words sinking in. The world they had known was unraveling, and their loved ones were no longer safe. She took a sip of the coffee, its warmth a bittersweet comfort as she tried to collect her thoughts.

Bruce leaned forward, his eyes locked onto Pippa's, a sense of urgency in his gaze. "Pippa, this is the reality we face now. We can't afford to be passive. We must take this seriously and consider protecting ourselves and those we care about before the situation escalates beyond our control."

Pippa nodded slowly, the gravity of the situation pressing down on her. She knew it was time to face this harsh reality head-on, to stand together and find a way to safeguard their loved ones. The coffee sat untouched between them, its warmth serving as a reminder that even in the darkest times, there was always a glimmer of hope, a chance to fight back against the looming threat.

With their determination and unity, they would navigate the treacherous path ahead and confront the danger that had infringed upon their lives, making a solemn promise to one another and their dear friend Sarah to uncover the truth and protect those they held dear.

Fear and concern replaced the anger that had consumed Pippa moments ago. She took a step closer to Bruce, their shared trepidation creating a temporary truce in their relationship. The need for unity and protection became their priority.

"Bruce, this is... this is terrible," Pippa whispered, her voice tinged with disbelief. "We need to be careful and take this seriously. The safety of everyone around us, including ourselves, is at stake."

Bruce nodded, his features etched with determination. "You're right, Pippa. We can't afford to ignore this. We must stay vigilant and do everything we can to ensure our safety and the safety of those around us."

Pippa's mind raced with questions and concerns. Who could be responsible for such violence? How could they protect themselves and others? They needed to act swiftly but also prudently.

"Let's gather any information we can, Bruce," Pippa suggested, her voice tinged with determination. "We need to stay informed and take necessary precautions. We should also contact the authorities and check on our loved ones."

Bruce nodded, appreciating Pippa's practical approach. "Absolutely. We should contact the police and see if they have any advice or updates. We should also inform our friends and family to ensure their awareness and safety."

As they both took out their phones and began making calls, a sense of solidarity formed between them. In the face of adversity, they realized the importance of supporting each other and setting aside their differences. They shared the common goal of safeguarding their lives and those of their loved ones.

As the sun continued to rise towards the PM, its gentle rays were now intermingled with a newfound determination. Pippa and Bruce set aside their arguments and embraced a united front against the encroaching darkness. They would navigate the uncertain times ahead together, drawing strength from each other and remaining resolute in their pursuit of safety and justice.

Pippa's words hung in the air, heavy with the weight of their tumultuous relationship and the harrowing events surrounding them. Her plea reflected a deep sense of vulnerability and a longing for a sense of stability and security.

Bruce, taken aback by the raw emotions in Pippa's voice, paused momentarily, his turmoil reflected in his eyes. The injunction laid bare the difficult choices they both faced, forcing him to confront the conflicts within himself.

As he looked at Pippa, he realized that their relationship had reached a critical juncture. The constant fear and uncertainty had taken a toll on both of them, straining the very foundations of their connection. Bruce understood the depth of Pippa's anguish and her need for reassurance, but he also grappled with his commitment to seeking justice and ensuring the safety of their community.

His voice was filled with sorrow and determination when he responded to Pippa's plea. "Pippa, I... I love you. But I also have a responsibility to protect others, to find answers, and to seek justice. It's not an easy choice, and I understand the toll it has taken on our relationship."

Bruce moved closer, his hand touching Pippa's trembling fingers. "I want nothing more than for us to find peace and a sense of security together. But we cannot ignore the dangers that exist. We need to strike a balance and address our fears while still fulfilling our obligations."

Tears streamed down Pippa's face as she struggled with her own conflicting emotions. The love she felt for Bruce was undeniable, but the constant state of fear had become overwhelming. She clung to the hope that they could find a compromise, a way to navigate their lives together without sacrificing their well-being.

"I don't want to lose you, Bruce," Pippa whispered, her voice filled with vulnerability and determination. "But we need to find a way to alleviate this constant fear, to create a space where we can both feel safe and secure. Can we work together to find that balance?"

Bruce nodded, his heart heavy realizing what was at stake. "Yes, Pippa, we can. We will find a way to navigate this storm together. We'll communicate more openly, seek support, and take steps to prioritize our well-being. I promise you, we'll find a way forward."

As their hands entwined, they understood that the road ahead would be challenging and that their journey would require compromise, understanding, and a shared commitment to healing. But they also knew their love for one another was worth fighting for. With that realization, they began rebuilding their relationship amidst uncertainty and danger.

As Bruce prepared to explain the significance of the case and the weight of his responsibility, Pippa interjected, her voice shaking with emotion and determination.

"I'm pregnant, Bruce," Pippa revealed, her words hanging in the air, carrying a profound sense of vulnerability and hope.

Bruce's breath caught in his throat as he absorbed the magnitude of Pippa's revelation. The conflicting emotions that consumed him moments ago paled compared to the overwhelming surge of love, joy, and responsibility that now washed over him.

He looked into Pippa's eyes, the weight of their connection deepening with this newfound knowledge. His voice trembled as he tried to find the right words. "Pippa, this changes everything. We have a life growing within us, a future that demands our attention and care."

Tears welled up in Pippa's eyes, a mixture of relief and uncertainty clouding her expression. "I know, Bruce. That's why I need to know that we can create a safe and stable environment for our children. The constant fear and danger surrounding us... I don't want our baby to grow up in that world."

Pippa's eyes glistened with tears, her smile reflecting their shared happiness. She had always imagined starting a family with Bruce, but the timing was far from perfect, considering the chaos surrounding them.

But then, her expression shifted, and her smile faded. She looked directly into Bruce's eyes, her voice taking on a more somber tone. "I know it should be a time of joy, but with everything that's been going on... the murders, the danger, the uncertainty... I can't help but feel overwhelmed. I'm unsure if I want our baby to grow up in such a mess, Bruce."

Bruce's smile gradually waned as he realized the depth of Pippa's concerns. He reached out and took her hand, his gaze filled with understanding. "Pippa, I understand your fears. This is a challenging time for both of us, and it's only natural to worry about our child's future. We have to prioritize their safety and well-being above all else."

Pippa nodded, a mix of relief and sadness in her eyes. She knew that making such a decision was not easy, and it didn't diminish their love for each other or their excitement about becoming parents. It was a choice driven by the desire to protect their child from the turmoil that had become their reality.

Bruce felt a wave of devastation crash over him as Pippa's words continued to reverberate in his ears. The crumbling of their relationship was a bitter pill to swallow, leaving him at a loss for words. He tried to find the proper response to salvage what remained of their connection, but the weight of their circumstances seemed impossible.

His voice trembled as he finally managed to speak, his heart heavy with sorrow. "But

Pippa, I... I don't want it to end like this. Please, let's talk about it. Let's find a way to work through this together."

Pippa's eyes glistened with unshed tears as she met Bruce's gaze, her voice laced with pain and resignation. "Bruce, it's not the end, but we've been through so much already. The constant fear, the uncertainty, the strain on our relationship... It's become too much to bear. I can't ignore my well-being and the well-being of our child any longer."

Tears welled up in Bruce's eyes as the reality of their crumbling love sank deeper. He had always known that their path was fraught with challenges, but he had held on to the hope that their bond could withstand anything. Now, he had to face the painful truth that their journey together had ended abruptly and heart-breakingly.

"I understand, Pippa," Bruce managed to say, his voice choked with emotion. "I never wanted our love to cause you pain. I'm sorry for the burden I've placed on you. I'll respect your decision, even though it breaks my heart."

Silence settled between them, punctuated only by the echoes of their shattered dreams. The morning sun, which had once symbolized new beginnings, now cast a gloomy light on their parting.

At that moment, Bruce and Pippa knew their paths had diverged; their once-shared future now split into separate directions. They stood there, enveloped in the weight of their emotions, unable to bridge the chasm that had grown between them.

With heavy hearts, they began the painful process of untangling their lives, each step an agonizing reminder of what they had lost. As they turned away, their hearts ached with the bittersweet memories of a love that had once burned brightly.

The afternoon sun continued its decent, oblivious to the shattered bond in its wake. Bruce and Pippa, once connected by love, now faced an uncertain future, forever changed by the fractures of their broken relationship.

Bruce stood there, his heart weighed down by a profound sense of loss. The realization that their paths had diverged, even beyond the context of the murder investigation, hit him with an overwhelming force. The future he had envisioned with Pippa seemed to crumble before his eyes, leaving him with a sense of emptiness and uncertainty.

He took a deep breath, steeling himself against the pain that threatened to consume him. Acceptance washed over him, albeit reluctantly, as he acknowledged that the challenges ahead encompassed the pursuit of justice and the task of rebuilding his life without Pippa by his side.

With a heavy heart, Bruce turned away from Pippa, knowing that it was time to face the difficult journey ahead on his own. The morning sun, now shining with a cruel irony, illuminated the path he now had to tread. Each step felt heavy as if the weight of their shattered relationship were imprinted on his every movement.

As he walked away, a mix of emotions churned within him—grief, longing, and a determination to find his sense of purpose and strength. Bruce knew that he had to focus on the investigation, bringing justice to the victims and ensuring the safety of others. But he also understood the need to heal his own heart, to mend the fragments of his shattered dreams.

In the quiet solitude of his thoughts, Bruce vowed to rediscover himself and rebuild his life, one step at a time. The road ahead would be challenging, and the pain of losing Pippa would linger, but he would persevere.

As the morning sun continued its ascent, Bruce found solace in the promise of new beginnings, however distant they seemed. He would carry the memories of his love for Pippa, cherishing them while finding the strength to move forward.

And so, with a mix of sorrow and determination, Bruce embarked on self-discovery and personal growth. The echoes of their fractured love reminded him of the depth of his emotions, but he remained hopeful that someday, in some way, their paths might converge again.

With a heavy heart and a resolute spirit, Bruce embraced the weight of his responsibilities. The personal turmoil he experienced threatened to consume him, but he knew that pursuing justice demanded his undivided attention.

Setting aside his heartache, Bruce channeled his energy into the murder investigation at the train station. The gravity of the crime weighed heavily on him, fuelling his determination to uncover the truth and ensure that the perpetrator faced the consequences of their actions.

Bruce faced numerous challenges and obstacles as he delved deeper into the investigation. The grim reality of the crime scene, the painstaking process of gathering evidence, and the arduous task of piecing together the puzzle tested his resolve. Yet he remained undeterred, driven by a commitment to justice and a desire to bring closure to the victims' families.

Days turned weeks and weeks into months as Bruce worked tirelessly, his focus unwavering. The personal wounds remained unhealed, but he pressed on, drawing strength from the knowledge that his efforts could make a difference in a world of darkness.

Along the way, Bruce encountered allies who shared his passion for justice. Together, they united against the forces of crime and injustice, lending support and camaraderie in the face of adversity. They became his confidants, his rock, helping him navigate the treacherous path he had chosen.

As the investigation unfolded, Bruce's tenacity began to yield results. Piece by piece, he unraveled the intricate web of deceit, slowly closing in on the truth. His pursuit of justice took him to unexpected places, and the revelations he uncovered were shocking and disheartening. But he refused to let despair consume him, channeling his emotions into a fierce determination to right the wrongs and ensure that justice prevailed.

Through the darkest moments, Bruce found solace in the knowledge that his work had a purpose and that his dedication could bring closure to those affected by the crime. He carried the weight of his shattered relationship with Pippa as a constant reminder of the sacrifices he had made along the way.

In the end, Bruce's unwavering resolve and tireless pursuit of justice bore fruit. The murderer was apprehended, and the truth was exposed to the light of day. Though scarred and changed, Bruce emerged from the experience with a renewed sense of purpose and a profound understanding of the fragility of life and love.

The chapter of his relationship with Pippa had closed, leaving behind heartache and uncertainty. Yet, as he continued his journey, Bruce carried their shared experiences, the lessons learned, and the memories they had once cherished. And though the road ahead remained uncertain, he knew that he had grown stronger, fuelled by a commitment to justice and resilience born from the ashes of lost love.

And so, with a heavy heart but an unyielding spirit, Bruce pressed on, ready to face the next chapter of his life, armed with the lessons learned and a determination to make a difference in a world that desperately needed it.

# CHAPTER ELEVEN

**B**ruce's mind was filled with determination and longing as he went to the club where Pippa worked undercover as a stripper. Despite the complexities and challenges of the case, he hadn't given up on their connection. He believed that their shared experiences and the bond they had formed were vital to unlocking crucial information and memories.

As Bruce entered the dimly lit club, the pulsating music and the seductive atmosphere enveloped him. He discreetly made his way through the crowd, searching for Pippa among the performers on the stage. His heart raced with anticipation, knowing that this encounter could be a turning point in their journey.

Finally, he spotted her moving gracefully on the stage, captivating the audience with her seductive dance. Bruce's gaze never wavered as he locked eyes with Pippa, hoping to ignite a spark of recognition and trigger their shared memories. After her performance, Bruce approached Pippa with nervousness and determination. He needed her to remember their past and understand the significance of their connection in the case context and how it had influenced his career as an investigator.

"Pippa," Bruce called softly, trying to capture her attention amidst the pulsating music and the club's noise. "It's me, Bruce. We've been through so much together. The case we worked on shaped my path as a private investigator. I need you to remember the moments we shared and the importance of what we uncovered."

He held his breath, hoping for a glimmer of recognition in her eyes, a flicker of remembrance that would reignite the flame of their shared journey. The weight of their connection and the revelations they had uncovered hung in the air, filling Bruce with a mix of hope and uncertainty.

As the club's music and chatter swirled around them, Bruce waited anxiously for Pippa's response, hoping their meeting in this unconventional setting would rekindle the memories that held the answers they sought.

Bruce's mind was pulled in two directions, torn between his desire to reconnect with Pippa and his relentless pursuit of the truth. The scarcity of fingerprints in recent murder cases had frustrated him, and he knew that Pippa's unique skills and knowledge could prove invaluable in this investigation aspect.

While he was slightly relieved that the Montebello PD had not responded to his Notice of Power Abuse directed towards Pippa's withdrawal from the County of Essex PD's investigations, he couldn't let it distract him from his current objective. The need for fingerprints had become increasingly urgent, and he believed that Pippa held the key to unlocking this crucial piece of the puzzle.

Bruce had to balance his intentions delicately as he approached Pippa in the club. He wanted to reignite their connection and remind her of their shared experiences, but he also needed her expertise in fingerprint analysis. He hoped she would be willing to assist him, even if it meant temporarily stepping away from her undercover role.

"Pippa," Bruce began, his voice soft yet determined, as he tried to find the right words to convey his intentions. "I know this may seem unconventional, but I need your help. The scarcity of fingerprints in these recent murder cases is hindering our progress. Your expertise in fingerprint analysis could be the missing piece we need to break through this barrier. I understand the importance of your undercover work, but I believe we can significantly solve these crimes."

He paused, giving Pippa a moment to process his words and consider his request. The weight of their past experiences and the gravity of the current investigation hung in the air, creating a sense of urgency and possibility.

"I know there are risks involved, and I don't want to jeopardize your position, but I believe that our partnership can yield important breakthroughs," Bruce continued, his voice filled with sincerity. "Please consider assisting me with fingerprint analysis. It could make all the difference in uncovering the truth and bringing justice to those responsible."

Bruce held his breath, hoping that Pippa would understand the importance of their collaboration and the impact they could have together. He knew that the decision ultimately rested in her hands, but he couldn't help but feel a glimmer of hope that their shared journey would continue and lead them closer to the answers they sought.

Bruce's heart skipped a beat as he witnessed the sudden intrusion of the black-suited men into the club. The atmosphere shifted from one of seductive allure to one of tension and danger. His gaze remained fixed on Pippa as he watched the men forcefully remove her and several other women from the premises.

Fear and concern coursed through Bruce's veins. This was not ordinary; it was a complete show of heart-pumping danger. The fact that Pippa was among those targeted intensified his sense of urgency and protectiveness toward her.

Without a moment's hesitation, Bruce sprang into action. Ignoring the chaos, he maneuvered through the crowd, determined to reach Pippa and ensure her safety. The instinct to shield her from harm fuelled his every step.

As Bruce approached the exit, he caught fleeting glimpses of the black-suited men shoving Pippa and the other women into waiting vehicles. Panic and worry surged within him, knowing that time was of the essence. He needed to act swiftly if he hoped to rescue Pippa and unravel the mystery behind this unexpected threat.

Drawing upon his resourcefulness and determination, Bruce formulated a plan. He would track the vehicles, follow the danger trail that had snatched Pippa away, and uncover the truth lurking beneath the surface. The journey ahead was uncertain, but Bruce was prepared to face whatever obstacles awaited him to protect Pippa and bring those responsible to justice.

As he stepped out of the club and into the night, adrenaline surged through Bruce's veins. The stakes had been raised, and the path ahead had become more treacherous. But fuelled by his unwavering determination and a newfound resolve, he embarked on a mission to rescue Pippa and confront the forces that sought to harm her.

The danger was palpable, but Bruce knew his pursuit of the truth and commitment to Pippa's well-being would guide him through the darkness. With every step forward, he would inch closer to unraveling the secrets that threatened their lives and finding the answers that had eluded them for so long.

Bruce's heart raced as Detective Elaine Murphy's car screeched to a halt before him. The anger of being unable to save Pippa and the other girls still coursing through his veins, he wasted no time and quickly hopped into the passenger seat.

"Detective Murphy," Bruce said, a mixture of relief and gratitude in his voice. "I wasn't expecting to see you here."

Detective Murphy smirked as she shifted the car into gear, her eyes focused on the road ahead. "Timing is everything, isn't it?" she replied cryptically.

Bruce couldn't help but wonder how Detective Murphy always appeared at the right moment, like a guardian angel watching over him. Her presence both intrigued and unsettled him, and he knew there was more to her involvement in the case than she had revealed.

As the car sped away from the scene, Bruce glanced at Detective Murphy, his eyes filled with determination. "We need to find Pippa and those who abducted her," he stated firmly. "They're connected to the larger conspiracy; we can't let them slip away."

Detective Murphy nodded, her focus unwavering. "Agreed. We're in this together, Bruce. I have my reasons for pursuing this case, and we need to work as a team to uncover the truth and bring justice to those involved."

Bruce felt a surge of renewed hope. Despite the dangers and setbacks they had encountered, he knew that with Detective Murphy by his side, they stood a better chance of overcoming the obstacles in their path.

Bruce's mind raced with questions and possibilities as the car sped through the city streets. The mysteries deepened, and the urgency to find Pippa and dismantle the web of deception intensified.

With Detective Murphy driving, their shared pursuit of justice propelled them forward, their determination unwavering. Together, they would navigate the treacherous twists and turns of the investigation, following the trail of danger and deceit until they reached the heart of the truth.

Little did they know that their partnership would unveil secrets far more sinister than they could have ever imagined, testing their resolve and challenging the very foundations of their beliefs. But they were prepared to face whatever awaited them, for the truth was their compass and justice their ultimate goal.

In the car, Bruce and Detective Murphy exchanged glances, their shared determination silently acknowledged. The road ahead was uncertain, but they were ready to confront the devil and expose the darkness threatening to consume them all.

# CHAPTER 12

B ruce's mind whirled with the lack of fingerprints around the murder victim, dampening his hopes of finding a breakthrough. The absence of evidence except the boy's fingerprints shattered the tenuous threads of optimism he had held onto.

Despite his involvement and past, Leonard Frost believed someone was targeting his family. He trusted the police, hoping they would do everything possible to protect his loved ones. Bruce understood the gravity of the situation and the urgency to uncover the truth and bring those responsible to justice.

But before proceeding with his investigation, Bruce knew he needed to speak with Detective Elaine Murphy. Her cryptic words echoed in his mind, "Every dog has its day." She understood the crime scene more deeply, having arrived before Bruce and potentially discovering crucial clues.

Bruce sought out Detective Murphy, driven by curiosity and a need for collaboration. He had to know what she had made of the crime scene and what insights she could offer. They had an unspoken connection, and he sensed that her perspective could illuminate the dark mysteries surrounding them.

As he approached Detective Murphy, Bruce's mind raced with questions. He would ask her about the supply fraud in the Forestry Department of Dream Farms, a potential lead that could unravel more secrets and expose a more extensive web of corruption. But he knew he had to approach her carefully, allowing her to answer at her discretion.

Bruce found Detective Murphy in a secluded corner of the crime scene, away from the commotion and prying eyes. Her expression was as inscrutable as ever, but

Bruce could sense an undercurrent of anticipation.

"Detective Murphy," Bruce began, his voice steady but laced with curiosity. "Your words, 'Every dog has its day,' have been echoing in my mind. I believe there's more to them than a mere idiom. What did you mean by that?"

Detective Murphy regarded Bruce with a measured gaze, taking a moment to choose her words carefully. "Bruce, the world of crime is complex, filled with layers of deception and hidden agendas. Sometimes, those who believe they hold all the power are unaware that their time will come, that the truth will eventually catch up to them."

She paused, her eyes searching Bruce's face for understanding. "In our pursuit of justice, we often encounter formidable adversaries, individuals who seem untouchable. But rest assured, no matter how elusive, every dog will face the consequences of their actions. We must be patient, persistent, and willing to dive deep into the shadows to uncover the truth."

Bruce nodded, his mind racing with possibilities. He could sense that Detective Murphy knew more than she let on, that she held a piece of the puzzle he had been desperately seeking. But he also understood that unraveling the truth would require patience and a willingness to face the darkness head-on.

"Detective Murphy, I'm committed to uncovering the truth, no matter how convoluted the path may be," Bruce declared, determination shining in his eyes. "I believe our paths have crossed for a reason, and together, we can shed light on the mysteries that have plagued us."

Detective Murphy's lips curved into a half-smile, a glimmer of respect shining in her eyes. "Bruce, you have shown remarkable tenacity and resourcefulness throughout this investigation. Your drive to seek justice is commendable. Let us continue to work together, trust in our abilities, and follow the present leads. In due time, the enigmatic pieces of this puzzle will come together, and the truth will be revealed."

As Bruce and Detective Murphy stood there, united in their pursuit of the truth, an unspoken understanding passed between them. They were both aware that the path ahead would be treacherous, but they were determined to press forward, unraveling the intricate web of secrets that had entangled them.

With renewed purpose, Bruce and Detective Murphy would face the challenges head-on, knowing that their shared determination and unwavering pursuit of justice would eventually lead them to the answers they sought. Their day of reckoning for those responsible drew near, and they were ready to seize it.

# CHAPTER 13

**B**ruce's mind was filled with determination and longing as he went to the club where Pippa worked undercover as a stripper. Despite the complexities and challenges of the case, he hadn't given up on their connection. He believed that their shared experiences and the bond they had formed were vital to unlocking crucial information and memories.

As Bruce entered the dimly lit club, the pulsating music and the seductive atmosphere enveloped him. He discreetly made his way through the crowd, searching for Pippa among the performers on the stage. His heart raced with anticipation, knowing that this encounter could be a turning point in their journey.

Finally, he spotted her moving gracefully on the stage, captivating the audience with her seductive dance. Bruce's gaze never wavered as he locked eyes with Pippa, hoping to ignite a spark of recognition and trigger their shared memories. After her performance, Bruce approached Pippa with nervousness and determination. He needed her to remember their past and understand the significance of their connection in the case context and how it had influenced his career as an investigator.

"Pippa," Bruce called softly, trying to capture her attention amidst the pulsating music and the club's noise. "It's me, Bruce. We've been through so much together. The case we worked on shaped my path as a private investigator. I need you to remember the moments we shared and the importance of what we uncovered."

He held his breath, hoping for a glimmer of recognition in her eyes, a flicker of remembrance that would reignite the flame of their shared journey. The weight of their connection and the revelations they had uncovered hung in the air, filling Bruce with a mix of hope and uncertainty.

As the club's music and chatter swirled around them, Bruce waited anxiously for Pippa's response, hoping their meeting in this unconventional setting would rekindle the memories that held the answers they sought.

Bruce's mind was pulled in two directions, torn between his desire to reconnect with Pippa and his relentless pursuit of the truth. The scarcity of fingerprints in recent murder cases had frustrated him, and he knew that Pippa's unique skills and knowledge could prove invaluable in this investigation aspect.

While he was slightly relieved that the Montebello PD had not responded to his Notice of Power Abuse directed towards Pippa's withdrawal from the County of Essex PD's investigations, he couldn't let it distract him from his current objective. The need for fingerprints had become increasingly urgent, and he believed that

Pippa held the key to unlocking this crucial piece of the puzzle.

Bruce had to balance his intentions delicately as he approached Pippa in the club. He wanted to reignite their connection and remind her of their shared experiences, but he also needed her expertise in fingerprint analysis. He hoped she would be willing to assist him, even if it meant temporarily stepping away from her undercover role.

"Pippa," Bruce began, his voice soft yet determined, as he tried to find the right words to convey his intentions. "I know this may seem unconventional, but I need your help. The scarcity of fingerprints in these recent murder cases is hindering our progress. Your expertise in fingerprint analysis could be the missing piece we need to break through this barrier. I understand the importance of your undercover work, but I believe we can significantly solve these crimes."

He paused, giving Pippa a moment to process his words and consider his request. The weight of their past experiences and the gravity of the current investigation hung in the air, creating a sense of urgency and possibility.

"I know there are risks involved, and I don't want to jeopardize your position, but I believe that our partnership can yield important breakthroughs," Bruce continued, his voice filled with sincerity. "Please consider assisting me with fingerprint analysis. It could make all the difference in uncovering the truth and bringing justice to those responsible."

Bruce held his breath, hoping that Pippa would understand the importance of their collaboration and the impact they could have together. He knew that the decision ultimately rested in her hands, but he couldn't help but feel a glimmer of hope that their shared journey would continue and lead them closer to the answers they sought.

Bruce's heart skipped a beat as he witnessed the sudden intrusion of the black-suited men into the club. The atmosphere shifted from one of seductive allure to one of tension and danger. His gaze remained fixed on Pippa as he watched the men forcefully remove her and several other women from the premises.

Fear and concern coursed through Bruce's veins. This was not ordinary; it was a complete show of heart-pumping danger. The fact that Pippa was among those targeted intensified his sense of urgency and protectiveness toward her.

Without a moment's hesitation, Bruce sprang into action. Ignoring the chaos, he maneuvered through the crowd, determined to reach Pippa and ensure her safety. The instinct to shield her from harm fuelled his every step.

As Bruce approached the exit, he caught fleeting glimpses of the black-suited men shoving Pippa and the other women into waiting vehicles. Panic and worry surged within him, knowing that time was of the essence. He needed to act swiftly if he hoped to rescue Pippa and unravel the mystery behind this unexpected threat.

Drawing upon his resourcefulness and determination, Bruce formulated a plan. He would track the vehicles, follow the danger trail that had snatched Pippa away, and uncover the truth lurking beneath the surface. The journey ahead was uncertain, but Bruce was prepared to face whatever obstacles awaited him to protect Pippa and bring those responsible to justice.

As he stepped out of the club and into the night, adrenaline surged through Bruce's veins. The stakes had been raised, and the path ahead had become more treacherous. But fuelled by his unwavering determination and a newfound resolve, he embarked on a mission to rescue Pippa and confront the forces that sought to harm her.

The danger was palpable, but Bruce knew his pursuit of the truth and commitment to Pippa's well-being would guide him through the darkness. With every step forward, he would inch closer to unraveling the secrets that threatened their lives and finding the answers that had eluded them for so long.

Bruce's heart raced as Detective Elaine Murphy's car screeched to a halt before him. The anger of being unable to save Pippa and the other girls still coursing through his veins, he wasted no time and quickly hopped into the passenger seat.

"Detective Murphy," Bruce said, a mixture of relief and gratitude in his voice. "I wasn't expecting to see you here."

Detective Murphy smirked as she shifted the car into gear, her eyes focused on the road ahead. "Timing is everything, isn't it?" she replied cryptically.

Bruce couldn't help but wonder how Detective Murphy always appeared at the right moment, like a guardian angel watching over him. Her presence both intrigued and unsettled him, and he knew there was more to her involvement in the case than she had revealed.

As the car sped away from the scene, Bruce glanced at Detective Murphy, his eyes filled with determination. "We need to find Pippa and those who abducted her," he stated firmly. "They're connected to the larger conspiracy; we can't let them slip away."

Detective Murphy nodded, her focus unwavering. "Agreed. We're in this together, Bruce. I have my reasons for pursuing this case, and we need to work as a team to uncover the truth and bring justice to those involved."

Bruce felt a surge of renewed hope. Despite the dangers and setbacks they had encountered, he knew that with Detective Murphy by his side, they stood a better chance of overcoming the obstacles in their path.

Bruce's mind raced with questions and possibilities as the car sped through the city streets. The mysteries deepened, and the urgency to find Pippa and dismantle the web of deception intensified.

With Detective Murphy driving, their shared pursuit of justice propelled them forward, their determination unwavering. Together, they would navigate the treacherous twists and turns of the investigation, following the trail of danger and deceit until they reached the heart of the truth.

Little did they know that their partnership would unveil secrets far more sinister than they could have ever imagined, testing their resolve and challenging the very foundations of their beliefs. But they were prepared to face whatever awaited them, for the truth was their compass and justice their ultimate goal.

In the car, Bruce and Detective Murphy exchanged glances, their shared determination silently acknowledged. The road ahead was uncertain, but they were ready to confront the devil and expose the darkness threatening to consume them all.

# CHAPTER 14

As Bruce raced through the city streets, hot on the trail of the suspects, he couldn't help but be amazed by Detective Elaine's driving skills. The chase was intense, adrenaline coursing through their veins as they weaved through traffic and decisively navigated sharp turns.

Detective Elaine's agility behind the wheel was unexpected, surpassing Bruce's expectations. Her swift maneuvers and calculated driving resembled that of a Formula One racer, displaying a level of skill and finesse that left him in awe.

Screeching tires and the blur of passing buildings filled the air as they closed in on their target. Bruce held on tight, his heart pounding with exhilaration and determination. He couldn't let the suspects escape after everything they had uncovered.

Through the twists and turns of the car chase, Bruce felt a newfound respect for Detective Elaine's abilities. She possessed a range of talents beyond what he had initially anticipated. Her presence in this investigation had proven to be more than a coincidence.

As they continued their high-speed pursuit, Bruce couldn't help but wonder about Detective Elaine's past, the experiences that had honed her skills and made her the formidable detective she is today. He knew there was much more to her than met the eye, and this car chase only scratched the surface of her capabilities.

During the adrenaline-fuelled chase, Bruce resolved to uncover the truth about Detective Elaine Murphy and her enigmatic presence in the investigation. He was determined to peel back the layers and discover the depths of her involvement, for he sensed that she held secrets that could bring them closer to the elusive truth they sought.

But for now, Bruce focused on the task during the exhilarating car chase. Together with Detective Elaine, they pursued the suspects with relentless determination, fuelled by their shared pursuit of justice and their unyielding desire to end the tangled web of mysteries that surrounded them.

The sudden arrival of Detective Christopher Hunter added another layer of intensity to the already adrenaline-fuelled car chase. The three-car fleet of the abductors weaved through the streets, pushing the limits of speed and agility as they raced towards their target.

Tensions reached a boiling point as the chase escalated, with Detective Elaine, Bruce, and Detective Hunter relentlessly pursuing the abductors. The streets became a battleground, each vehicle vying for control in a high-stakes race against time.

But just as the chase seemed to peak, the abductors unleashed a deadly trap. The road ahead was strewn with steel caltrops, sharp spikes designed to puncture tires and halt the pursuit. Detective Elaine reacted swiftly and tried to evade the dangerous obstacles, but the sudden maneuver caused the car to lose control.

In a harrowing twist of fate, the car flipped and crashed into a nearby eatery. The impact resonated through the air with a loud crash. Bruce's heart raced as he realized the gravity of the situation. The pursuit had come to an abrupt and catastrophic halt.

As the dust settled and sirens filled the air, Bruce and the detectives emerged from the wreckage, shaken but determined. They assessed the damage, knowing that time was of the essence. The abductors were still on the loose, and their ultimate objective remained mysterious.

Gathering their wits and pushing through the physical and emotional toll, Bruce,

Detective Elaine, and Detective Hunter reaffirmed their commitment to the mission. Despite the setback, their resolve remained unyielding. They would regroup, strategize, and continue their pursuit, determined to bring down the abductors and uncover the truth behind the sinister plot that had led them to this point.

The crash had left its mark, both physically and mentally, but it hadn't extinguished the fire burning within their hearts. With a renewed sense of urgency, Bruce and the detectives prepared to resume their pursuit, knowing that the road ahead would be treacherous but unwilling to let any obstacle deter them from their mission.

The hunt for answers continued, fuelled by their unwavering determination and a shared commitment to justice. They would overcome the challenges, rise from the wreckage, and push forward, determined to see the truth prevail.

As the dust settled and the reality of the crash set in, Detective Christopher Hunter quickly assessed the situation. Recognizing the immediate need for assistance, he made the selfless decision to abandon the pursuit and rushed to aid Detective Elaine and Bruce.

Together, they worked swiftly to ensure the safety of everyone involved. With the wreckage surrounding them, Detective Christopher Hunter and Detective Elaine carefully extricated Bruce from the car, ensuring he was unharmed.

Bruce couldn't help but mutter a string of curses under his breath, his frustration mounting. He knew he could have done better, and now Pippa was gone. The stakes had been higher than ever, and the pursuit had turned into a desperate race against time.

As they waited for the medic, Christopher called for an ambulance. The wailing sirens grew louder, and soon, the ambulance pulled up, its flashing lights piercing through the darkness. Christopher helped Bruce to his feet, supporting him as he staggered toward the paramedics.

Just as they were about to load Bruce into the ambulance, a figure emerged from the alley across the street. It was Pippa, disheveled and battered but unmistakably alive. She approached the group, her voice laced with a hint of mischief.

"Miss me?" Pippa's words hung in the air, causing a momentary hush over the scene. Bruce's astonishment was palpable. He didn't know whether to get angry or relieved, his emotions in turmoil. He cast his gaze at Pippa, his voice a mix of disbelief and concern. "Pippa, what on earth were you doing at that club? You were supposed to be away, safe."

Pippa crossed the road to join them, her face a mixture of determination and weariness. She embraced Bruce, and he winced, a sharp jolt of pain shooting through his broken arm.

"Bruce," Pippa began her voice grave, "I had a lead. I couldn't sit idly by and distract you with what I'd found. If I'd told you, you wouldn't have been able to get to where you were tonight. I had to follow it through."

As the medic bandaged Bruce's wounds, the group shared a quiet conversation. Bruce's heart was relieved at Pippa's unexpected return, but he couldn't help but worry about her safety. The night he had been dangerous for all of them.

The paramedics eventually declared that Bruce was fit to go, though he would require further care in the coming days. Together, they made their way down to Christopher's house, where they could take a moment to regroup and process the tumultuous events.

In the chaos that ensued, Bruce realized that Pippa, the key to unraveling the mysteries that had plagued him, was still with them. Determined not to let her fall into the wrong hands again, they swiftly decided to take Pippa with them.

Their paths had intertwined unexpectedly, and Pippa held vital information that could shed light on the larger conspiracy at play. With their renewed commitment to uncovering the truth, Bruce, Detective Elaine, Detective Christopher Hunter, and Pippa became a united front bound by a shared objective.

The challenges ahead remained daunting, but Bruce knew they stood a better chance of overcoming the obstacles in their path. With Pippa's knowledge and the combined skills and determination of the three detectives, they formed a formidable team ready to face whatever lay ahead.

As they regrouped and prepared to resume their pursuit, Bruce couldn't help but feel a surge of hope. The crash may have momentarily disrupted their plans but hadn't extinguished their resolve. They would press forward, driven by the need to uncover the truth, bring the abductors to justice, and protect Pippa from further harm.

With their minds focused and their resolve fortified, the team embarked on the following investigation phase. They knew that the challenges awaiting them would test their limits, but they were fuelled by a shared determination to bring justice to those responsible for the crimes that had plagued their lives.

Bruce, Detective Elaine, Detective Christopher Hunter, and Pippa formed an unlikely alliance, each bringing unique skills and perspectives. They recognized that their strength lay in their unity, relying on their combined expertise and unwavering trust.

Their journey took them deep into the city's underbelly, following leads, analyzing evidence, and connecting the dots that would eventually lead them to the heart of the conspiracy. They encountered dangerous individuals, confronted their fears, and weathered the storms of doubt and uncertainty.

Throughout their quest, they uncovered dark secrets that shook them to their core, revealing a web of corruption and power that extended far beyond their initial suspicions. The investigation grew in scope, intertwining with larger criminal enterprises and exposing a network of influential figures who had operated with impunity for far too long.

Yet, even in the face of adversity, the team persisted. They strategized, collaborated, and relied on their collective intelligence to navigate the treacherous paths they traversed. Every setback and obstacle only fuelled their determination to uncover the truth and ensure justice prevailed.

As they delved more deeply, the team realized the importance of striking a delicate balance between their personal lives and the demands of the investigation. They leaned on one another for support, finding solace in their shared understanding of their weight and their sacrifices to pursue truth.

Days turned into weeks, but their resolve remained unyielding. With each breakthrough, they grew closer to the heart of the conspiracy, unraveling the threads that bound together the criminal underworld and the secrets that threatened to tear their lives apart.

In the end, their collective efforts paid off. Though painful, the truth emerged from the shadows, exposing the culprits and their intricate web of deceit. The powerful were brought to their knees, and justice was served.

The team that emerged from the investigation was forever changed. The bonds they forged in the face of adversity had grown more substantial, and their shared experiences had shaped them into formidable allies. Their journey had been arduous, but they had emerged victorious, united by a common purpose and a relentless pursuit of justice.

As they parted ways, their paths diverging once again, they carried with them the memories of their shared triumphs and the knowledge that their collective efforts had made a difference. The impact of their actions would ripple through the lives of many, leaving behind a legacy of courage and resilience.

And so, as they ventured into the following chapters of their lives, their spirits remained unbroken. They had confronted the unknown, exposed the darkness, and emerged as beacons of justice in a world that often teetered on the edge of chaos.

Their journey may have ended, but their commitment to truth and justice endured, a flame that would continue to burn brightly in their hearts. And should the need arise, they would once again rise to the challenge, ready to confront the unknown and expose the forces that threatened the world they fought to protect.

# CHAPTER 15

B ruce wasn't physically hurt but needed a long rest. As a PSTD patient, he needed this ritual if he were to get up strong again. He worried about Pippa and what could occur to her.

After the intense events and the toll it took on Bruce, he recognized the importance of caring for himself physically and mentally. Aware of his struggles with PTSD, he knew that rest and self-care were vital for his recovery and resilience.

Bruce found solace in a peaceful retreat where he could temporarily escape the chaos that had consumed his life. Surrounded by nature, he allowed himself time to decompress, to heal the emotional wounds that had been reopened during the recent events.

During his rest, thoughts of Pippa lingered in Bruce's mind. He worried about her safety and the unknown perils she might be facing. But he also knew he needed to prioritize his well-being to help her. It was a tricky balance, but one he understood was necessary. As the days passed, Bruce immersed himself in therapeutic activities, seeking solace in the tranquility of the surroundings. He engaged in mindfulness exercises, practiced deep breathing techniques, and took moments to reflect on his experiences.

Through therapy and self-reflection, Bruce gradually came to terms with the lingering effects of his PTSD. He learned coping mechanisms to manage the anxiety and intrusive thoughts that sometimes overwhelmed him. He understood that healing was a gradual process that required patience, self-compassion, and the support of others.

While Bruce focused on his recovery, he remained vigilant about Pippa's well-being. He maintained contact with the rest of the team, exchanging updates and sharing any leads or information that could aid in keeping an eye on her. He trusted in their collective efforts to help him with that.

With each passing day, Bruce felt a renewed strength and clarity growing within him. The rest and self-care had replenished his reserves, allowing him to face the challenges ahead with a stronger resolve.

When the time came for Bruce to re-join the investigation, he did so with a revitalized spirit. He knew Pippa's safety depended on their collective efforts and was ready to lend his skills and determination to the cause.

As he stepped back into the fray, Bruce carried the lessons learned during his restful period. He understood the importance of self-care and its impact on his ability to navigate the complexities of the case. And while the path ahead remained uncertain, he was prepared to face whatever challenges lay in wait, knowing that his resilience had been fortified through the essential ritual of rest.

The atmosphere inside Christopher's house was tense as Bruce sat, awaiting the nurses' arrival for his final treatment. The room was quiet, filled with an underlying sense of apprehension. Elaine and Christopher exchanged glances, their skepticism apparent as they anticipated the nurses' arrival.

A knock on the door shattered the stillness, causing Christopher to furrow his brow. "They've come pretty early," he mused, turning to Elaine for confirmation.

Elaine's eyes mirrored Christopher's uncertainty as she nodded. "Yes, it does seem a bit soon. Let's be cautious."

Christopher approached the door cautiously, his senses on high alert. He cracked it open to reveal two nurses standing on the doorstep, their smiles seemingly benign.

The nurses greeted Christopher with friendly professionalism. "Good afternoon, sir. We're here to administer the final dosage for Mr. Bruce's treatment."

Christopher squinted, scrutinizing the nurses. He had become skilled at reading people, and something about these nurses set off alarm bells. "I don't recognize either of you. Where are the regular nurses?"

The nurses maintained their smiles, their demeanor unwavering. "The regular nurses are on leave, so we were instructed to take their place for today. No need to worry, sir. We're here to ensure Mr. Bruce receives his treatment as planned."

Reluctantly, Christopher allowed them inside. The last nurse slammed the door shut as they entered with a resounding thud. Elaine gasped in surprise, her eyes widening with alarm. Christopher spun around, his heart pounding.

Before he could react, the second nurse, devoid of the earlier smile, launched a vicious kick at Christopher. The impact sent him flying across the room, and he crashed into a glass coffee table, shattering it into a thousand pieces. The room echoed with his agonized scream.

"Marge, stay inside!" Christopher shouted to his wife, summoning all his strength to stand up and face their attackers. His body ached from the impact, but he was determined to protect his wife and friends.

The two nurses' demeanors, now entirely different, removed their nurse uniforms to reveal black combat outfits beneath. They were not nurses but assassins, and their mission was to eliminate anyone in their way.

One of the assassins darted toward the guest room where Bruce was resting.

Elaine, filled with terror, tried to block her path, but the other assassin intercepted her, and a showdown ensued. The room had transformed from a place of care and recovery into a battlefield.

Elaine, driven by adrenaline and desperation, took a stance to fight. The two women grappled with each other, the assassin's strength and training pitted against Elaine's determination to defend an injured Bruce.

Meanwhile, Christopher, still recovering from his injuries, moved between the guest room and the approaching assassin to stop two from going after Bruce. He knew his strength alone might not be enough, but he would do whatever it took to keep the other threat away from Bruce. At least Bruce could handle one.

In the guest room, Bruce stirred, sensing the turmoil outside. He knew he needed to act, but his broken arm rendered him defenseless. He searched for any object that could be used as a weapon, hoping to even the odds.

The battle inside Christopher's house had escalated into a life-and-death struggle, with every participant aware that the outcome of this confrontation would determine not only their fate but also that of their dear friend Bruce.

Detectives Christopher and Elaine immediately acted as the attacker disguised as a nurse approached. They swiftly assessed the situation, their instincts honed by years of experience in law enforcement.

Detective Christopher positioned himself between the attacker and Bruce, his gaze focused and his body poised for sudden movements. Detective Elaine, equally alert, stood by his side, ready to provide backup and support.

The attacker, undeterred by the detectives' presence, advanced with an air of confidence. But the detectives were prepared. They had faced dangerous situations before and were well-trained to handle such threats.

As the attacker lunged forward, intent on reaching Bruce, Detectives Christopher and Elaine acted in perfect synchronization. Christopher deftly blocked the attacker's path, using his training to anticipate her movements and counter her attempts to get past him.

Elaine, utilizing her quick reflexes and combat skills, swiftly moved to restrain the attacker, using techniques to immobilize and disarm her.

Inside the room was a different ball game. As Bruce observed the nurse's suspicious actions, he realized he needed to act swiftly to protect himself. With his keen senses heightened by the adrenaline coursing through his veins, he carefully gauged the timing and the moment to make his move.

As the nurse approached with the syringe, Bruce feigned a sudden shift in his sleep, subtly repositioning himself to create an opportunity. With his eyes narrowed, he tracked her every movement, ready to react immediately.

Simultaneously, his frustration grew upon realizing that the gun he had seen Detective Christopher place under his pillow had mysteriously vanished. Bruce knew he couldn't rely on the weapon to defend himself; he would have to rely on his resourcefulness and quick thinking.

As the nurse leaned closer, preparing to inject him, Bruce seized the moment. He swiftly reached out with a burst of energy, aiming to disarm her and gain control of the situation. His years of training and instincts kicked in as he utilized his knowledge of self-defense to his advantage.

In a split second, Bruce's hand intercepted the nurse's wrist, forcefully redirecting the syringe away from his arm. He swiftly disarmed her with strength and technique, rendering her unable to carry out her nefarious intentions.

Bruce wasted no time subduing the nurse, securing her until backup arrived. He knew this encounter was just another piece of the puzzle, revealing the depths of the danger surrounding him and the investigation.

As he restrained the nurse, Bruce's mind raced with questions. How did she know about his arm? Who sent her? And most importantly, what was her connection to the larger conspiracy they were unraveling?

The detectives swiftly secured the area once the immediate danger had passed, ensuring no other accomplices were lurking nearby. They communicated with their fellow officers, alerting them to the situation and requesting backup to investigate the incident further.

As the chaos settled, Bruce, though shaken by the sudden attack, felt a deep sense of gratitude for the swift action taken by Detectives Christopher and Elaine. Their presence saved him from harm and reminded him of the trust and camaraderie they had developed through their shared experiences.

With the situation under control, the detectives remained vigilant, recognizing that the threat they faced was part of a larger conspiracy. They understood that they needed to delve deeper into the investigation to uncover the motives behind the attack and the individuals responsible.

Bruce, grateful for the protection and support he had received, renewed his determination to assist the detectives in their pursuit of justice. He recognized that the case had become more personal than ever, and the safety of those involved, including Pippa, depended on their unwavering commitment to exposing the truth.

United by their shared mission and the dangers they faced, Bruce, Detective

Christopher, and Detective Elaine regrouped, ready to face the challenges ahead. They knew the road beforehand would be treacherous, but their resilience and unwavering resolve would guide them through the darkness as they sought justice for those who had fallen victim to the shadows.

Bruce's frustration transformed into determination, fuelling his relentless pursuit of the truth. The gun's disappearance served as a reminder that forces sought to hinder their progress, but he refused to be deterred.

With the situation under control, Bruce signaled to Detective Christopher and Detective Elaine, informing them of the encounter and the potential danger. Together, they strategized their next moves, using this unexpected turn of events as a catalyst to deepen their investigation and uncover the hidden truth within the shadows.

Their unity and unwavering resolve became their greatest strength as they pressed forward. They knew that the road ahead would be challenging, but they were determined to prevail for the sake of justice, and for those whose lives had been affected by the web of deceit, they were determined to untangle.

Breathing heavily but relieved, Bruce provided a detailed account of the events that had transpired to a set of police who had now reached the scene.

He emphasized the urgency of capturing the nurse's accomplices and uncovering the truth behind their actions.

The arrival of assistance marked a turning point in the investigation. The team now had a new lead, a captive who could shed light on the larger conspiracy.

As the nurse was apprehended and the room returned to a state of order, Bruce, Detective Christopher, and Detective Elaine shared a moment of relief. They understood that the road ahead would continue to be treacherous, but their perseverance and unity had proven effective once again.

With the support of the newly arrived reinforcements, they would delve deeper into the investigation, determined to bring those responsible to justice and ensure the safety of themselves and others at risk.

As they regrouped, Bruce's focus remained unwavering. He knew that every fight, every obstacle, and every step forward brought them closer to the truth. And with each victory, the resolve to protect Pippa and unravel the mystery strengthened, propelling them further into the heart of the darkness that threatened their lives.

As they gathered evidence and sought answers, Bruce, Detective Christopher, and Detective Elaine recognized the gravity of their embroiled situation. They were now more committed than ever to navigating the treacherous path ahead, inching closer to uncovering the dark secrets that had entangled their lives.

The events of that day would leave a lasting impact on their investigation, reminding them of the stakes involved and the lengths they would have to go to ensure that justice prevailed. The team would forge ahead, united by their shared purpose and the unwavering determination to unravel the truth, no matter the challenges ahead.

Detective Christopher's emotions ran high after the shocking turn of events. As he processed the situation, conflicting feelings battled within him. On one hand, he couldn't deny that Elaine's decisive action had saved Bruce's life, potentially preventing a tragedy. On the other hand, he felt a twinge of guilt for not reacting quickly enough to avoid the dire situation from escalating to that point.

In the immediate aftermath, a heavy silence enveloped the room as the weight of the situation settled upon them.

Detective Christopher's anger and frustration simmered just beneath the surface, directed at the nurse and, to some extent, himself for not acting faster.

Simultaneously, Elaine grappled with the gravity of her actions. Despite her swift response that undoubtedly averted a potential disaster, she too was shaken by the consequences of her choice. The reality that her bullet could have hit Bruce instead weighed heavily on her conscience.

As the team regrouped, the tension between Detectives Christopher and Elaine lingered, unspoken yet palpable. Both individuals recognized their complex emotions—gratitude, guilt, anger, and the shared understanding that they were all operating in a high-stakes environment.

Understanding the need for resolution and reconciliation, Bruce intervened, still recovering from the harrowing experience. He acknowledged the conflicting emotions and the intense pressure they were under, urging Detectives Christopher and Elaine to set aside their differences for their shared mission.

Realizing the truth in Bruce's words, Detective Christopher gradually softened his stance, recognizing that Elaine's actions, however difficult to accept in the heat of the moment, had ultimately saved Bruce's life. Elaine, in turn, acknowledged the gravity of the situation and expressed remorse for the potential consequences her actions could have had.

In the face of a relentless adversary, they understood the need for unity and trust. They realized that their pursuit of justice and the safety of their loved ones required them to put aside personal grievances and work together as a cohesive team.

In the aftermath of this crucial turning point, Detectives Christopher and Elaine began to rebuild the trust and camaraderie that had been momentarily shaken. Their determination to uncover the truth and bring those responsible to justice prevailed over their differences.

United once again, they reaffirmed their commitment to the investigation, vowing to delve deeper into the labyrinth of deceit and danger that surrounded them. The unexpected events only solidified their resolve to uncover the dark secrets and protect those at risk.

As they continued, Bruce, Detective Christopher, and Detective Elaine understood that their journey would be arduous and fraught with challenges and unforeseen obstacles. Yet, they remained steadfast in their pursuit, knowing their collective strength and unwavering determination would guide them through the shadows and toward the ultimate truth.

# CHAPTER 16

The aftermath of the intense confrontation in Christopher's house left a trail of shattered furniture and frayed nerves. As the dust settled, Christopher guided Bruce outside for a crucial conversation. The night air was filled with tension, mirroring the turmoil that had unfolded inside.

Christopher cleared his throat, his gaze fixed on Bruce. "Before this attack, Bruce, we collaborated with Pippa to gather information at the Stationelle club. We didn't tell you because we weren't sure how you'd react, but it was a joint effort to uncover more clues."

Bruce's anger flared, and he couldn't contain his frustration. "You let Pippa go to that dangerous place alone, especially when pregnant? Are you out of your mind, Christopher?"

Christopher bowed his head, filled with remorse. "I'm sorry, Bruce. It was a mistake, and I should have been more cautious. We thought we could keep her safe, but it was a risk we shouldn't have taken."

Bruce, still seething, eventually calmed down enough to ask, "How is Pippa now? Is she all right?"

Christopher hesitated for a moment, his gaze somber. "Bruce, I have to tell you something. Pippa has been abducted again."

Bruce's temper flared once more, his voice raised in frustration. "What? How could you let this happen, Christopher?"

Christopher tried to soothe his friend, understanding the anguish in Bruce's voice. "I know it's hard to accept, but we've received information that the club owner knows something. When night falls, we'll see to it. We're doing everything we can to find Pippa."

Though still angry, Bruce accepted the plan, knowing they had to take action. He turned away and walked off, the anger in his steps echoing his inner turmoil.

Christopher watched him go, his heart heavy with worry and regret. He sighed deeply, covered his face with his hands for a moment, and swiped a nearby barrel out of frustration. He silently prayed that they would find Pippa and bring her back safely. The night was far from over, and they were determined to do whatever it took to reunite with their missing friend.

The neon lights of the Stationelle club bathed the city's nightlife in a mesmerizing glow. The thumping bass reverberated through the streets as people lined up to enter the vibrant venue. Bruce, Christopher, and Elaine stood at the entrance, their purpose clear – to find answers about Pippa's whereabouts.

As they entered the club, the atmosphere was electric. The dance floor pulsed with energy as revelers moved to the beat of the music, their laughter and chatter mixing with the DJ's hypnotic tunes. The club was a maze of flashing lights, a dizzying dance of colors that painted the night.

They navigated through the crowd to reach the owner, a suave, sophisticated man with charm and charisma. He welcomed them with a warm smile and a wave of his hand. "Welcome to Stationelle, my friends! I trust you'll have a fantastic night here."

Christopher wasted no time, his voice solemn and determined. "We're not here to party. We need to know where Pippa is. You know her – red hair, pale skin, freckled face. Have you seen her?"

The club owner's smile wavered, but he maintained his composure. "I'm sorry, I don't know who you're talking about. We have a lot of guests, and it's a busy night."

Christopher persisted, his description more detailed. "She's our friend, and she's been here recently. We need to find her. She's in danger."

The owner's demeanor shifted, but he maintained a façade of indifference. "I can't help you with that. This is a place for enjoyment and celebration. You should relax and enjoy the night. Let's head to the upper section, where the view is breathtaking."

The owner's invitation seemed more of a distraction than genuine hospitality. Christopher was not one to be easily dissuaded. "We don't have time to enjoy the night. We need to find Pippa. Tell us where she is."

The owner refused to budge despite Christopher's persistence, his composure unshaken. "I've told you, I don't know her. Now, let's not waste this night. The upper section is calling. Join me, and perhaps your friend will turn up later."

Reluctantly, they followed the club owner to the upper section of the club. The view from there was breathtaking, with the city's dazzling lights stretching below them. Yet, the scene's beauty was marred by their mission's urgency.

The club pulsed with life as the night continued, a vibrant spectacle of revelry and decadence. Bruce, Christopher, and Elaine had no choice but to play along, their eyes scanning the crowd for any sign of Pippa. They couldn't afford to let their guard down in this labyrinth of lights, music, and unknown dangers.

The night had just begun, and they were determined to uncover the truth about Pippa's disappearance, no matter what it took.

Tensions mounted, and desperation grew as time went on, and they had gotten nowhere with the knowledge of Pippa's whereabouts. Detective Christopher's impulsive actions surprised everyone. Frustrated by the lack of cooperation from the club owner, he resorted to extreme measures, firing a warning shot into the winery.

The gunshot reverberated through the air, shattering the silence that had enveloped the scene. The club owner's eyes widened in fear and shock, realizing the gravity of the situation. The bullet had pierced a nearby wine barrel, causing the rich red liquid to spill onto the floor.

Detective Elaine and Bruce stood frozen, stunned by the sudden escalation. They knew such actions could have severe consequences and hinder their investigation. However, they also understood the mounting urgency to locate Pippa and uncover the truth behind the intricate web of deceit surrounding them.

With a mixture of fear and determination, the club owner finally cracked under the pressure. Realizing the severity of the situation, he revealed a crucial piece of information—a secret location known only to the higher echelons of the criminal underworld, where Pippa might have been taken.

The revelation ignited a renewed sense of purpose within the team. They understood that time was of the essence and couldn't afford to hesitate or second-guess their actions any longer. With the club owner's information, they embarked on a perilous journey to rescue Pippa and bring down the shadowy forces threatening their lives.

As they delved deeper into the dark side of the County of Essex, the team faced even greater dangers and challenges. They encountered ruthless individuals and met unexpected twists and turns along the way. However, their unwavering resolve and the bond forged through their shared experiences propelled them forward, determined to overcome every obstacle.

The journey ahead would test their courage, resilience, and loyalty. But with the lives of their loved ones hanging in the balance, they remained undeterred. United in their mission, Bruce, Detective Christopher, and Detective Elaine pushed forward, ready to confront the darkness head-on and rescue Pippa from the clutches of those who sought to harm her. The final battle loomed, and the team braced for the ultimate showdown. This battle would determine Pippa's fate and expose the truth behind the intricate corruption and deceit that had plagued the County of Essex for far too long.

Realizing the importance of the information they had obtained, Bruce, Detective Christopher, and Detective Elaine knew they had to tread carefully in pursuing the retired General. With the language barrier in mind, they quickly arranged for a skilled interpreter to facilitate communication during their encounter with the retired General.

Equipped with the necessary resources and a renewed sense of determination, they embarked on the journey to Westside, where the retired General was rumored to reside. The neighborhood was known for its close-knit community, vibrant culture, and fair share of secrets and dangers.

Upon reaching the retired General's residence, they were greeted by a weathered and dignified figure, the weight of his years apparent in his stooped posture and lined face. The interpreter stepped forward, bridging the gap between languages and enabling effective communication between the team and the retired General.

With the interpreter's assistance, they explained their visit's purpose and their mission's urgency. They sought information about Pippa's whereabouts and any connections the retired General might have to the shadowy forces they had been investigating.

Though initially guarded, the retired General recognized the determination in their eyes and the gravity of the situation. In hesitant yet revealing words, he began to share fragments of his knowledge, unraveling the intricate tapestry connecting Pippa to the County of Essex's dark underbelly.

As the conversation progressed, a clearer picture emerged. The retired General had once held a position of influence and power, operating in the shadows, and his involvement in illicit activities had earned him a notorious reputation. His connection to the case ran more profound than anyone could have anticipated.

The interpreter played a crucial role in bridging the language gap and the cultural nuances between the team and the retired General. Through their assistance, the team could navigate the complexities of the conversation and extract valuable information that would aid them in their mission.

With the retired General's cooperation, the team now possessed a vital piece of the puzzle. Armed with new leads and a clearer understanding of the criminal network's inner workings, they prepared to take the next bold steps in their quest for justice and the rescue of Pippa.

As they left the retired General's residence, the weight of their discoveries hung heavy in the air. They knew they were edging closer to the heart of darkness, where the true orchestrators of the County of Essex's criminal underworld awaited. But with their determination unyielding and their bond unbreakable, they pressed forward, ready to face the challenges ahead and secure Pippa's safety. As the team continued their investigation, the frustration of hitting dead ends grew. Fake car plate numbers proved a significant setback, making it challenging to trace the abductors and gather valuable leads. However, a glimmer of hope emerged when the man they were interrogating made a phone call in Spanish.

Detective Elaine, who had proven her linguistic skills earlier, quickly snapped her attention to the conversation, attempting to catch any vital information that could aid their search for Pippa. Bruce and Detective Christopher, intrigued by the sudden turn of events, watched with anticipation, hoping for a breakthrough.

After the call ended, Elaine's expression shifted from focused determination to disappointment. She explained to Bruce and Christopher that the conversation provided useless information. The man had spoken cryptically, perhaps aware of the potential consequences of revealing too much over the phone.

Frustration and concern crept into their minds as they grappled with the realization that they were again faced with a seemingly insurmountable obstacle. The man's conversation had raised more questions than answers, leaving them at a crossroads in pursuing Pippa. Undeterred, Bruce, Christopher, and Elaine knew they had to regroup and re-evaluate their strategy. The road ahead seemed even more treacherous, but their determination to find Pippa and bring the perpetrators to justice remained unwavering.

They understood that overcoming this setback would require a combination of resourcefulness, intelligence, and persistence. The team would have to delve deeper into the shadows, uncover hidden connections, and gather information from alternative sources to fill in the gaps left by the unproductive phone call.

With their collective expertise and unwavering commitment, Bruce, Christopher, and Elaine prepared to tackle the next phase of the investigation. They knew that even the most minor lead could be the key to unraveling the mystery and safely bringing Pippa back.

As they left the interrogation room, their minds brimming with possibilities and unanswered questions, they were resolved to continue the search, knowing that their determination and resilience would be crucial in overcoming the obstacles ahead. Bruce's heart leaped with relief and excitement as he received an unexpected text from Pippa. The message contained a location, "0234 Route Bonaventura, Montebello," providing a beacon of hope in their search for her.

Without wasting a moment, Bruce quickly shared the information with Detective Elaine and Detective Christopher. Their eyes met, mirroring the intensity of their shared purpose. The time for action had arrived.

They mobilized swiftly, aware that every passing second could be crucial. Bruce, Detective Elaine, and Detective Christopher hurriedly made their way to Route Bonaventura in Montebello, their senses heightened and their determination bolstered by the newfound lead.

As they reached the location, it was a large warehouse not used in years. Dusty floors, deprecating walls, and rusted irons were evidence of abandonment; their eyes scanned the surroundings, searching for any signs of Pippa or the presence of the abductors. The tension in the air was palpable as they cautiously advanced, each step guided by their shared mission and the bond they had forged in their relentless pursuit of the truth.

The location held its mysteries, shrouded in shadows and uncertainty. The team remained alert, their instincts honed to detect any danger that might lie ahead. They knew they were entering a potentially hazardous situation, but their unwavering resolve propelled them forward.

Silently, they moved through the area, their senses attuned to even the slightest sound or movement. With each passing moment, the weight of their anticipation grew, knowing they were drawing closer to the moment when their paths would intersect with Pippa's again.

Suddenly, amidst the quiet, they heard a faint cry for help. Their hearts raced as they followed the sound, their steps quickening. And then, in the dimly lit corner of the warehouse, they found her.

Pippa was battered and frightened but alive.

Emotions swelled within Bruce as he rushed to her side, his relief mingling with a renewed determination to bring those responsible to justice. The team stood united, embracing Pippa's rescue as a testament to their unwavering commitment and the strength they found in one another.

As they helped Pippa to safety, they knew their work was far from over. The mysteries and dangers that had plagued them throughout their investigation still loomed, demanding resolution and accountability. But now, with Pippa rescued and their spirits reignited, they were more determined than ever to uncover the truth and protect those they held dear.

The journey had been arduous, filled with obstacles and unexpected turns, but their shared purpose and unyielding bond had carried them through. As they looked ahead, their eyes glimmering with resolve, they knew that no matter the challenges that awaited them, they would face them together, united in their pursuit of justice and a brighter future.

# **CHAPTER 17**

As Bruce, Detective Elaine, Detective Christopher, and Pippa stood inside the vast warehouse, they scanned the surroundings, taking in the magnitude of the space before them. The dimly lit interior echoed with the mystery and possibilities that lay within its expansive walls.

The warehouse seemed like a blank canvas, waiting to be filled with purpose and meaning. It held the potential for a game—a game that could become their own, with rules shaped by their experiences, skills, and determination.

Bruce's mind started to churn with ideas; the thrill of the unknown fuelled his imagination. He knew that within this vast space, they had the opportunity to turn the tables on their adversaries, to create a strategic advantage that could lead them closer to uncovering the truth.

Bruce envisioned the warehouse as their playing field, drawing inspiration from the gaming world. He saw it as a place to set traps, devise strategies, and outsmart their opponents. It became a realm where their collective abilities and ingenuity would reign supreme.

Together, they started exploring the warehouse, searching for potential advantages and resources to aid them in their quest. They discovered hidden nooks, stacked crates, and a labyrinth of corridors, each offering the potential for strategic positioning and surprise attacks.

With their minds buzzing with possibilities, they began establishing rules within this game of pursuit and justice. They designated safe zones, planned escape routes, and identified areas where they could set up surveillance and gather crucial information.

The warehouse became their training ground, where they honed their skills and coordinated their efforts. They practiced tactical maneuvers, shared their knowledge and expertise, and developed a deeper understanding of their roles within the game they had created.

But amidst the excitement of their self-designed game, they remained vigilant, knowing that their real dangers were not confined to their established rules. The stakes were high, and the threats they encountered were unpredictable and formidable.

As they delved deeper into the vastness of the warehouse, their determination grew, fuelled by their shared purpose and the bond they had forged. They knew their game was not just about gaining an advantage but protecting the innocent, seeking justice, and ending the dark forces that had plagued their lives.

They found a physical space and a symbolic realm within the warehouse where their courage, intellect, and resilience would be tested. They embraced the challenges ahead, knowing that their game was not just for themselves but for all those who had suffered at the hands of the perpetrators they sought to bring down.

And so, with their self-created rules and the warehouse as their playground, Bruce, Detective Elaine, Detective Christopher, and Pippa prepared to face whatever lay ahead. Their game was no longer just a game—it was a battle for truth, justice, and the restoration of peace.

In this vast warehouse, their destinies would converge, and their actions would shape the course of their journey. With their hearts united and their spirits ablaze, they stepped forward, ready to face the challenges that awaited them, determined to emerge victorious in their quest for justice.

Bruce understood the delicate balance they needed to maintain to keep Pippa safe. Their enemies had the right to believe that Bruce, Detective Elaine Murphy, and Detective Christopher

Hunter held valuable information or leverage that could be used to their advantage. It was this misconception that would become their greatest strength.

Bruce devised a plan with a calm resolve, keeping their self-imposed rules in mind. They would play the enemies' hunger games, playing by their rules.

Bruce understood that every move they made needed to be strategic, calculated, and executed precisely. He kept a keen eye on the enemies, observing their behavior and looking for weaknesses or opportunities that could be exploited. He used his investigative skills to gather information discreetly, making mental notes of their patterns and vulnerabilities. Bruce's main objective was to keep a low profile, buy time, and ensure the enemies never knew of their presence while formulating their plan. He had an inside man whom he had convinced from within to engage them in conversation, subtly probing for information and using his wit to keep them off balance. At the same time, he maintained constant communication with Bruce, Detective Elaine, and Detective Christopher, conveying vital information and coordinating their efforts.

As the days passed, Bruce carefully observed the layout of the location where the other woman, who had been captured alongside Pippa before she escaped, was being held. He noted the guard rotations, the security measures, and potential weaknesses in the captors' defenses.

One crucial element of their plan was ensuring the captors never suspected their true intentions. Bruce remained cautious, always playing his role convincingly, even as he meticulously gathered any tools or resources that could aid in their escape.

Finally, the moment they had been waiting for arrived. They had gathered enough information and devised a plan that maximized their chances of success.

With the captors momentarily distracted, Bruce, Detective Elaine, and Detective Christopher sprang into action.

Utilizing their unique skills and working in perfect synchronization, they neutralized the captors one by one, swiftly and silently. Their combined training, knowledge, and determination proved to be a formidable force.

Ultimately, they rescued the women, ensuring their safety and ending the captors' reign of terror. The abductors never saw it coming, underestimating Bruce's and his team's resourcefulness and unwavering determination.

With the women safe, they emerged victorious in their mission from the confines of the captors' domain. They had adhered to their rules, outsmarted their adversaries, and reunited the women with the freedom they desperately needed.

Though the game was over, their journey was far from finished. They knew dark forces were still at play, and their fight for justice would continue. But they had proven they were a force to be reckoned with—a team bound by loyalty, resilience, and an unyielding commitment to the truth.

As they left the shadows of the captors' lair behind, Bruce, Detective Elaine, Detective Christopher, and Pippa walked into the light, ready to face whatever challenges lay ahead, knowing their unity and unwavering resolve would guide them through the darkest days.

The successful rescue operation left a sense of accomplishment in Bruce, Detective Elaine, and Detective Christopher. With the captors neutralized, they ensured the safety of the women who had been held captive for far too long. The location had been cleared, and their adversaries had underestimated their unwavering determination to see justice served.

As they emerged from the confines of the captors' lair, they knew that their journey was far from finished. Dark forces were still at play, and their fight for justice would continue. They walked into the light, ready to face whatever challenges lay ahead, united by their loyalty, resilience, and unyielding commitment to the truth.

But as they regrouped and breathed a sigh of relief for a job well done, Bruce's phone rang. His countenance changed as he listened to the voice on the other end, his expression increasingly tense.

The voice on the phone acknowledged Bruce's recent success, praising his ability to do away with the captors and free the captured people. But then, the tone grew sinister as the voice issued a chilling threat. "If you want Pippa to live, you'll do as I say."

Bruce's eyes darted toward Pippa, a look of deep concern in his eyes. The voice on the phone seemed to read his thoughts. "I see you're looking at her now, Mr. Bruce. My crosshairs are right on her forehead. It would be in your best interest to comply with my demands."

Christopher, sensing Bruce's distress, asked what was happening. Bruce raised his hand, a gesture for him to hold off, his attention entirely focused on the voice in his ear.

The voice on the phone laid out a series of instructions that Bruce would need to follow. Reluctantly, Bruce complied, aware that Pippa's life hung in the balance. He began walking backward as instructed, his gaze scanning the area, trying to pinpoint where the voice behind the phone was coming from.

The night had taken a dark and sinister turn, and Bruce knew he had no choice but to follow the orders to ensure Pippa's safety. The chilling threat had shifted the balance of power, and they were once again caught in a challenging game, their every move dictated by an unseen and dangerous adversary.

The voice over the telephone continued to issue instructions, demanding compliance from Bruce. He listened carefully, taking note of each demand while also searching for any clues that could lead to the person's identity on the other end of the line.

Bruce followed the instructions cautiously, understanding that his actions could mean the difference between life and death for Pippa. He moved purposefully, fulfilling each task while looking for any opportunity to gain the upper hand.

Bruce used his training and instincts to assess the situation as he fulfilled the demands. He scanned the surroundings, looking for any possible weaknesses or tools that could aid in their escape. Every moment counted, and he couldn't afford to miss any opportunity to turn the tide in their favor.

Meanwhile, Detective Elaine Murphy and Detective Christopher Hunter positioned themselves strategically, ready to act momentarily. They maintained constant communication with Bruce, ensuring they were in sync and prepared to assist him when the time was right.

Bruce's mind raced as he contemplated the motives behind the person orchestrating this twisted game. He analyzed their words, tone, and subtle hints that could provide insight into their true identity. He knew that uncovering the truth was crucial for their escape and bringing the mastermind to justice.

As Bruce continued carrying out the instructions, he devised a plan of his own, which involved outsmarting the voice on the other end of the line. He knew that he had to anticipate their next move, to think several steps ahead and turn the tables on them.

With each passing moment, Bruce's determination grew more robust. He refused to let fear consume him or cloud his judgment. Pippa's safety depended on his ability to stay focused, to remain calm under pressure, and to outwit their captor.

Finally, the moment arrived. Bruce had gathered enough information, observed enough patterns, and devised a plan that could tip the scales in their favor. With a combination of wit, courage, and the element of surprise, he made his move.

In a swift and calculated action, Bruce disarmed their captor, freeing Pippa from the restraints that held her captive. Together, they fought back, using their collective strength to overcome their adversary.

The voice on the other end of the line fell silent, their power over them broken. Bruce, Pippa, Detective Elaine, and Detective Christopher stood victorious, their bond more muscular than ever.

As they walked away from the vast warehouse, leaving behind the remnants of their ordeal, Bruce knew that their journey was far from over. They had triumphed in this battle, but battles were still to be fought, truths uncovered, and justice served.

With Pippa safely by their side, Bruce and his team were ready to face whatever challenges lay ahead, united in their commitment to protect the innocent and bring down those who sought to inflict harm.

Their shared experience had forged an unbreakable bond that would guide them through the darkest times and propel them forward in their pursuit of justice. Together, they were a force to be reckoned with, ready to confront any obstacle that stood in their way.

Bruce, Pippa, Detective Elaine, and Detective Christopher cautiously observed a group of individuals as they resurfaced near the heap of containers. Three hefty men and the tall lady with a punk hairstyle presented a formidable presence, and the air was thick with tension.

The lady stood out among the group with her athletic physique and commanding presence. It was clear that she was the leader, exuding confidence and authority. Bruce's instincts told him that she was someone not to be underestimated.

As they approached, the lady's piercing gaze locked onto Bruce, her expression unreadable. Bruce could sense a mixture of curiosity and challenge in her eyes. They had stumbled upon an unexpected confrontation, and the stakes were high.

Detective Elaine and Detective Christopher positioned themselves alongside Bruce and Pippa, their collective readiness evident. The dynamics shifted, and the atmosphere crackled with intense energy as both sides assessed each other, trying to discern their intentions.

Without a word, the lady stepped forward, her presence commanding attention. Bruce prepared himself for any possible scenario, racing to strategize their next move. He couldn't afford to let his guard down, not when the safety of his team and the truth they sought hung in the balance.

Finally, the lady broke the silence, her voice strong and authoritative. She revealed herself as Victoria, a prominent figure in the criminal underworld, and she made it clear that she had been observing their actions closely. She spoke of power, influence, and a hidden agenda intertwined with their justice pursuit.

Bruce, ever vigilant, listened intently, analyzing her words and trying to gauge her true motives. He knew they had stumbled upon a complex web of deceit and corruption, and Victoria seemed to hold the key to unraveling the truth.

With measured caution, Bruce responded, his voice steady and firm. He sought to understand Victoria's role in the larger scheme of things and how she fit into the puzzle they were piecing together. He needed to determine whether she was an ally, a foe, or a potential source of vital information.

The standoff continued, both sides locked in a tense negotiation of words and intentions. Each step and each dish had the potential to shift the balance of power. Bruce remained resolute, driven by his unwavering determination to uncover the truth and protect those he cared about.

In this precarious moment, the lines between friend and foe blurred, and alliances could be forged or broken. Bruce knew he had to tread carefully, using his intuition and wit to navigate the intricate dance of power and deception.

As the conversation unfolded, Bruce sensed a glimmer of common ground, a shared objective hidden beneath the layers of suspicion. He recognized that Victoria held valuable information that could aid them in their quest for justice, and she seemed willing to offer a fragile truce.

With cautious optimism, Bruce extended an invitation for collaboration, a proposition to work together to dismantle the web of corruption that ensnared them all. The path ahead remained uncertain, but Bruce was determined to seize every opportunity to bring the truth to light and ensure the safety of those he held dear.

The standoff between the two sides gradually dissolved, replaced by a tentative alliance born out of necessity and a shared desire for justice. The journey ahead would be treacherous and riddled with challenges, but together, they would confront the darkness and strive to uncover the hidden truths in the shadows.

As Bruce, Pippa, Detective Elaine, Detective Christopher, and Victoria prepared to embark on this uncertain path, their collective strength and determination provided a glimmer of hope. They would face their adversaries head-on, ready to fight for justice, expose the hidden agendas, and ultimately, bring the guilty to their knees.

Bruce's mind whirled as the voice uttered those haunting words. They echoed through his thoughts, triggering memories and emotions from his past. It was a phrase etched into his psyche long ago, a painful reminder of the injustices he had witnessed and experienced.

He couldn't help but be transported back to when he was a young boy surrounded by poverty and violence. Growing up in a neighborhood plagued by crime, he saw first-hand how some individuals were denied essential opportunities and chances in life.

The voice's cryptic message brought forth memories of the faces he had encountered, the innocent lives cut short, and the systemic flaws perpetuating inequality and despair. It was a stark reminder of the deep-seated issues he had committed to fighting against.

As Bruce grappled with the weight of those memories, he realized that this encounter was not merely coincidental. The voice had chosen those words deliberately, knowing their impact on him. It was a deliberate attempt to stir his emotions, to challenge his convictions, and to test his resolve.

With a newfound determination, Bruce turned to face the voice, filled with conviction. "Not everyone deserves a chance," he mutters, his words carrying the weight of his experiences and the injustice he had witnessed. "It's not for us to judge who deserves or doesn't deserve a chance. It's our responsibility to fight for justice, to advocate for the voiceless, and to allow everyone to rise above their circumstances."

At that moment, Bruce realized that this encounter was not only about rescuing Pippa or unraveling their investigation's mysteries. It was a battle for something greater—equality, fairness, and the belief that every life held inherent value.

With his resolve strengthened, Bruce and his team pressed on, driven by a renewed sense of purpose. They would continue their pursuit of justice, refusing to let the darkness consume them. Guided by their shared conviction, they would challenge the notion that not everyone deserved a chance and strive to create a world where equal opportunities were within reach.

As they ventured deeper into the unknown, Bruce carried the weight of his past experiences and the words of the voice with him. They would be a constant reminder of the injustices that must be confronted and the battles yet to be fought. And with every step forward, Bruce vowed to be a beacon of hope, determined to make a difference in a world where everyone truly deserved a chance.

# CHAPTER 18

In the quiet solitude of his office, Detective Bruce found himself drowning in the sea of paperwork that had become his daily routine. Eight years had passed since the fateful incident haunted him, and he was determined to make the best of his chance for redemption.

Across town, Detective Christopher Hunter, Bruce's trusted partner, was in a separate location, laying low and monitoring the surroundings. Their communication was precise and discreet, a testament to their years of partnership. The time had come to act, and they had to do it right.

Their plan was set in motion. They had a culprit to capture.

When Christopher saw some sneaky movements, he notified Bruce, who left his office and followed him into a large building. The culprit had walked in with a group of men.

Bruce and Christopher slithered in, and when they were sure they would not miss, they split and fired; a chill ran down their spines as they discovered their guns were empty. Laughter echoed through the hall, and their blood ran cold. The threat was not from an unknown adversary but from one of their own.

Detective Elaine Murphy made her presence known with a dramatic entrance, accompanied by Pippa and two other men. The strange woman by her side sent shivers down their spines, and the voice of Adams Gibson, Chief of the County of Essex's PD, rang through the room, confirming their darkest suspicions.

As the plot unraveled, the truth became shockingly plain. Pippa and Elaine were siblings, but their roles were far from ordinary. Elaine had been suspended from the Montebello PD two weeks before the crimes began, setting her on a treacherous path.

Pippa was positioned as a honey trap for Bruce, drawing him into their twisted web. The actual murderer was none other than Kia, who had attacked Bruce in the past, but she was just a pawn in this elaborate game.

It was Elaine who had orchestrated the murders, implanting Leonard Austin Frost Leonard's DNA at the scene. The team's objective was to use the case to expose a long-running fraud. Unfortunately, it came at the cost of Leonard George's son's life.

Kia, as had the two men and the two disguised nurses at Christopher's house, had been hired. But what shocked Bruce the most was the revelation that Pippa, Elaine, and Chief Gibson were all part of the same family.

The Chief had a vendetta fuelled by grief. He had just two sons, and they were the two Spanish teenagers Bruce had killed eight years ago, the incident that set all of this in motion. Now, the Chief sought revenge, patiently waiting for the right moment to unleash his fury. That was when it all clicked to Bruce.

Bruce had a brother who died of a drug overdose after years of depression. He lived with a memory that haunted him till the point of death. He led a team of robbers to rob his parents, who refused to support his insane dream of running an illegal arms wing with some Russian dealers. He knew his father had the money but didn't give it out.

The Russians forced him to rob his father. But at the scene, his father recognized the scar on his upper wrist and called his name. Scared that the father might get him jailed, he shot him dead. His mother must have died of a heart attack shortly after that, even before being shot by one of the Russians.

Bruce watched the clip with a mix of shock and determination. It appeared that

~ 270 ~

someone had tampered with the webcams, likely in an attempt to monitor his activities or gain unauthorized access to his personal information. Realizing his privacy had been violated only strengthened his resolve to uncover the truth.

With the Russians responsible for stealing money from his father now out of reach, Bruce understood that he needed to find another source of funds to continue his pursuit of justice. The drug deal involving two Spanish teenagers was his last chance to gather the necessary resources.

However, Bruce knew that getting involved in a drug deal carried significant risks and potential consequences. He carefully evaluated the situation, weighing the potential benefits against the inherent dangers. He considered the legal implications, the safety of those involved, and the potential impact on his investigation.

Bruce realized that his primary goal was to bring those responsible for targeting him and stealing from his family to justice. He gathered more information about the drug deal, the individuals involved, and its potential risks.

He used his investigative skills to dig deeper into the backgrounds of the Spanish teenagers and any connections they might have to the criminal underworld. He contacted his network of informants and contacts, seeking insights and advice on how to proceed.

Bruce understood that his actions needed to be calculated and well-planned. He sought to minimize the risks and ensure the safety of everyone involved, including himself. He established secure communication channels, conducted thorough background checks, and assessed the credibility and reliability of the information he received.

While desperate for the funds to continue his investigation, Bruce also remained mindful of the ethical implications of his actions.

He strived to uphold the law and maintain his integrity despite adversity. He balanced his motivations with the pursuit of justice, ensuring his actions would not compromise the goal of holding those responsible accountable.

Bruce meticulously built his case and prepared for the drug deal with each step. He knew this endeavor carried significant risks, but he was determined to use every opportunity to bring justice to his family and himself.

But even before the buyers arrived, Bruce intercepted them. As a SAS, combating them wasn't hard. He killed the two Spanish teenagers and shot his brother in the leg.

Bruce wanted to kill him with the same gun he used to kill their parents. But he wanted to have a word with him first.

Bruce never saw him until he served his term and later died of an overdose.

Bruce still recalled what he had said to the Spanish teenagers before killing them.

Not everyone deserves a chance!

That was where the game all started!

Bruce's realization that someone was after his life sparked his newfound determination. He recognized the importance of uncovering the truth behind the attack and delving into the incident's root cause. This revelation fuelled his commitment to investigating the case with unwavering resolve.

Bruce began meticulously gathering information, piecing together the puzzle of events leading up to the attack on his family. He dug deep into his past, reaching out to old contacts and investigating any potential connections that might shed light on the motive behind the assault.

Bruce's investigation took him deep into the underbelly of this clandestine network as he tirelessly unraveled the intricate web of deception and corruption. The more he delved into the case, the clearer it became that his family's attack was just the tip of the iceberg, connected to a series of other crimes and conspiracies.

He uncovered evidence linking high-ranking officials, influential people in business, and shadowy organizations to the orchestrated attacks. These individuals operated in the shadows, manipulating events to serve their interests while remaining undetected by the public eye.

As Bruce dug deeper, he faced numerous challenges and encountered powerful adversaries who sought to protect the secrecy of the network at all costs. He received threats, discovered attempts to discredit him, and faced dangerous situations that tested his resolve.

But Bruce's commitment to uncovering the truth and seeking justice for his family remained unwavering. He utilized his investigative skills, resources, and network of trustworthy allies to navigate the treacherous landscape and expose those responsible for the crimes.

Bruce pieced together the puzzle with each breakthrough, revealing a complex network of political corruption, illicit activities, and undercover operations. He discovered that the motivations behind the attacks were multi-faceted, driven by greed, power struggles, and the desire to maintain control over various sectors of society.

Bruce understood that the fight against this network went beyond seeking justice for his family. It became a mission to expose the truth and protect innocent lives from further harm. He meticulously documented his findings, gathering concrete evidence to ensure those involved would be held accountable for their actions.

Throughout his investigation, Bruce encountered whistle-blowers and insiders who, driven by guilt or a desire for redemption, provided crucial information that shed light on the network's operations. He also collaborated with law enforcement agencies, journalists, and others who shared his commitment to dismantling this web of deceit.

As Bruce uncovered the extent of the conspiracy, he knew he would need to be strategic and cautious. He took precautions to protect himself and those close to him, aware that his pursuit of the truth had made him a target. Trust became a precious commodity, and he carefully chose whom to confide in, ensuring that his actions remained concealed from those who might seek to undermine his efforts.

Bruce's relentless pursuit of the truth eventually led him to the heart of the clandestine network, where he confronted its masterminds and unveiled their true intentions. In doing so, he brought justice to his family and exposed the network's operations to the world, leaving an indelible mark on the fight against corruption and deception.

The web of deception Bruce uncovered involved domestic and foreign actors, blurring the lines between legal and illegal activities. He found connections to influential figures in politics, business, and organized crime, suggesting a complex and dangerous alliance.

With each revelation, Bruce realized the extent of the threat facing his family and the wider community. He understood that the motives behind the attack went beyond personal vendettas or disagreements. There were forces at play that sought to manipulate and control the balance of power for their gain.

Bruce's determination to bring justice to his family and expose the network grew stronger. He meticulously documented the evidence he uncovered, building a case to bring down those responsible and dismantle the entire network.

As he delved deeper, Bruce encountered resistance and faced mounting danger.

Bruce did not quickly shake down the individuals involved in the network, and they sought to protect their interests at any cost. Bruce realized that he needed to be cautious, navigating the treacherous waters of this complex web while ensuring his safety.

His investigation took him to different corners of the world, chasing leads and confronting influential individuals. He formed alliances with trusted allies and leveraged his skills and resources as best he could. Bruce understood that he needed to stay one step ahead of his adversaries to succeed.

Through his relentless pursuit of the truth, Bruce exposed the intricate workings of the network. His findings threatened the individuals and the systems that allowed them to thrive. The revelations sparked public outrage, forcing authorities to take action and bring the perpetrators to justice.

In the end, Bruce's commitment and unwavering determination paid off. The complex web of deception was unraveled, and those responsible for the attack on his family were held accountable. The exposure of the network sent shockwaves through society, serving as a stark reminder that even the most powerful can be brought down by the relentless pursuit of truth and justice.

As he delved deeper into the intricate tapestry of corruption, Bruce discovered a network of influential individuals involved in the heinous act that took his loved ones away. Politicians, business magnates, and even members of law enforcement seemed to be entangled in a vast conspiracy designed to protect the guilty and hide the truth.

But Bruce was undeterred. He knew that exposing such influential figures would not be easy, and it would require him to

operate outside the confines of the law
Honing his physical and mental abilities
he transformed himself into a symbol of
fear for those who preyed upon the
innocent. He became the Dark Knight, a
vigilante who would stop at nothing to
bring justice to the corrupt.

With each new revelation, Bruce's resolve
grew more assertive. The pain and
anguish that haunted him after the
tragedy now fuelled his relentless pursuit
of those responsible. He saw himself as a
beacon of hope for a city consumed by
crime and corruption, a symbol that even
the most powerful were not beyond the
reach of justice.

Bruce's journey was not without its
challenges. He faced danger at every turn
risking his life and sanity to confront the
darkness that enveloped his city. But his
unwavering determination, unparalleled
intellect, and physical prowess allowed
him to overcome the obstacles in his path.

Ultimately, Bruce's relentless pursuit paid off. He gathered enough evidence to expose the culprits and reveal the true extent of their crimes. He orchestrated their downfall with the help of dedicated allies, ensuring they faced the total weight of the law.

In the end, Bruce's family's tragic fate served a greater purpose. Their loss catalyzed his transformation into a force for good, a symbol of justice that inspired others to stand up against corruption. Through his unwavering determination and indomitable spirit, Bruce had turned tragedy into a crusade that would leave a lasting impact on the world he sought to protect. Bruce returned to the present, and his instincts kicked in as Pippa raised her gun. He realized that this was the end of the line, and Pippa shot him in the leg. The emergency ambulance arrived as Bruce lay on the ground, and it seemed like it was all over.

But Christopher had seen through their plan from the beginning. He knew Elaine was responsible for taking the gun out of its holster. Bruce punched his watch in a desperate move, sending it hurtling towards Kia. The device exploded with a blinding flash, disorienting their enemies. A sniper on the warehouse roof came to their aid, taking down Pippa. Elaine was shot in the leg, and the showdown between her and Bruce began. It was a brutal and intense fight, and in the end, Bruce put a bullet in her chest, ending the chaos she had orchestrated.

As battered and bruised as he was, Christopher faced off against the Chief, who had fought fiercely to avenge his sons. The battle was intense, but Christopher's Special Forces training and determination propelled him forward. He outmaneuvered the Chief, exploiting every opportunity to land precise strikes.

Ultimately, Christopher incapacitated the Chief, ensuring he would no longer pose a threat. The SWAT team from Montebello PD arrived, and together, they secured the area and provided medical attention to those in need.

Christopher's bravery and skill played a pivotal role in controlling the situation, and his actions were celebrated as a testament to his courage and dedication.

When the culprits were apprehended, they were taken to different police stations. The complex web of deceit had been untangled, but the scars of that night would remain forever.

In the aftermath of the confrontation, Bruce and Christopher were left to reflect on the past and the darkness they had faced. The truth had been unveiled, and justice had been served, but the memories of that night would linger, a constant reminder of the thin line between duty and deception.

The long-buried secrets had resurfaced, and the truth had finally seen the light of day. But the shadows of the past would forever haunt them, a testament to the complexities of the human heart and the darkness that could reside within even those closest to us.

# CHAPTER 19

**Bruce and Christopher sat behind in the hall, taking in what they had passed through.**

B ruce is at the forefront, having loved Pippa wholeheartedly. There, he wondered if she was genuinely pregnant with his child as she claimed. It became more transparent to him how she always got caught and found a way to return. He laughed at himself for being delusional.

Just as they sat, a mysterious figure came forth. The one behind the calls as he introduced himself.

With their hearts pounding and adrenaline coursing through their veins, Bruce and Detective Hunter steeled themselves to confront the enigmatic figure who had descended into the hall. Their determination to uncover the truth remained unyielding despite the uncertainty.

As the figure stepped forward, a dim light revealed a tall, imposing silhouette shrouded in darkness. Their voice carried an air of authority and an undertone of menace as they addressed Bruce and Detective Hunter.

"I've been watching your every move," the figure declared, their voice filled with an unsettling calmness. "You think you can expose the truth? You're merely pawns in a game far bigger than you can comprehend."

Bruce and Detective Hunter exchanged a glance, their resolve unshaken. They had come too far to be deterred now. His voice steady and resolute, Bruce responded, "We've seen the corruption that plagues this city. We won't rest until justice is served."

The figure let out a chilling laugh. As the laughter echoed in their ears, a shiver ran down Bruce and Detective Hunter's spines, causing a momentary ripple of unease. The evil presence of the enigmatic figure sent a palpable wave of fear and apprehension coursing through their bodies.

Bruce's instincts sharpened his senses on high alert. He could feel the weight of the impending danger, the lurking darkness that threatened to engulf them. Yet, instead of succumbing to fear, he channeled the shivers into a renewed resolve.

Though momentarily shaken, Detective Hunter steadied himself, his eyes reflecting determination. He refused to let fear cloud his judgment or deter him from pursuing justice. The shivers served as a reminder of the stakes at hand, fuelling his determination to expose the truth. "Justice is a facade, a comforting lie for the weak-minded. The real power lies in those who control the strings. You're nothing but insects caught in their web."

Bruce's eyes narrowed, his determination deepening. "We may be caught in their web, but we'll find a way to unravel it. No matter the cost."

Detective Hunter stepped forward, his voice echoing with conviction. "We're not alone in this fight. Others believe in justice and are willing to stand up against corruption. You can't silence us all."

The figure observed them silently, their gaze piercing through the darkness. Then, with disdain, they spoke, "Very well. You may continue your futile crusade. But remember, the deeper you delve, the greater the darkness you'll uncover. And in the end, it may consume you."

Bruce and Detective Hunter stood their ground, undeterred by the figure's warning. Both were prepared to face whatever darkness lay ahead, for they knew that the truth they sought was worth the sacrifices they might make.

Bruce and Detective Hunter reaffirmed their commitment to their cause as the figure retreated into the shadows. With unwavering determination, they prepared to embark on the next phase of their journey, ready to confront the depths of deception and fight for justice, no matter the consequences.

# THE END

Printed in Great Britain
by Amazon

31074856R00161